"Y OU H

"You don't have to sound so surprised," he said. "Everyone has something that could bring them to their knees." He could see the uncertainty growing in her eyes. Did she honestly think he was so inhuman as not to have a weak spot?

"What's yours?" she asked.

Should he lie or tell the truth? Was she ready to hear the truth? Somehow he had the feeling she would never be ready to hear the truth, yet it was beyond him to lie to her.

"You are my weakness."

"Me?"

"Yes, you."

"I don't understand."

How could she be so blind? Didn't she realize what she did to him? He was tired of trying to explain it all to her.

"Maybe this will show you what I'm talking about." He hauled her into his arms and claimed her mouth with the fierce need that had been building for years.

WHAT ARE *LOVESWEPT* ROMANCES?

They are stories of true romance and touching emotion. We believe those two very important ingredients are constants in our highly sensual and very believable stories in the LOVE-SWEPT line. Our goal is to give you, the reader, stories of consistently high quality that may sometimes make you laugh, sometimes make you cry, but are always fresh and creative and contain many delightful surprises within their pages.

Most romance fans read an enormous number of books. Those they truly love, they keep. Others may be traded with friends and soon forgotten. We hope that each LOVESWEPT romance will be a treasure—a "keeper." We will always try to publish

LOVE STORIES YOU'LL NEVER FORGET
BY AUTHORS YOU'LL ALWAYS REMEMBER

The Editors

Loveswept ® *803*

SECOND-TIME LUCKY

MARCIA EVANICK

BANTAM BOOKS
NEW YORK · TORONTO · LONDON · SYDNEY · AUCKLAND

SECOND-TIME LUCKY

A Bantam Book / September 1996

ISBN 0-553-44561-8

Published simultaneously in the United States and Canada

Bantam Books are published by Bantam Books, a division of Bantam Dou-
bleday Dell Publishing Group, Inc. Its trademark, consisting of the words
"Bantam Books" and the portrayal of a rooster, is Registered in U.S.
Patent and Trademark Office and in other countries. Marca Registrada.
Bantam Books, 1540 Broadway, New York, New York 10036.

PRINTED IN THE UNITED STATES OF AMERICA

OPM   0 9 8 7 6 5 4 3 2 1

DEDICATION

To Elizabeth Barrett,

Finding a great editor is more precious than gold. With you, I hit the mother lode.

Thanks for believing.

PROLOGUE

"Really, Mother! This is your emergency? You made me fly two thousand miles to tell me Dayna took the boys camping?" Luke Callahan shook his head at his tearful mother and paced back toward the French door overlooking the formal gardens. Night had fallen on this quiet upscale neighborhood of Denver where he had grown up. He had left his home outside of Washington, D.C., before dinner to catch the next plane to Colorado. He was now hungry, tired, and totally exasperated with Eileen Beatrice Callahan. Her tears had long ago ceased to affect him.

"She didn't take them to one of the national parks, Luke. She took them to Aces High."

Luke turned at that announcement. His sister-in-law had taken his nephews to an abandoned ghost town, not one of the heavily populated tourist parks she usually frequented? "What in the world did she take them there for?"

"She told me she wanted the boys to see their inheritance, and"—Eileen shuddered in disgust—"she wanted them to have some fun and an adventure while they panned for gold."

Luke raised an eyebrow. "They're panning for gold?" No wonder his poor mother was frantic. Imagine the scandal that would cause at the country club. Eileen Callahan's adored grandsons were panning for gold like common scavengers. Searching for nonexistent nuggets seemed harmless to him, but a woman and two small boys staying alone in a ghost town could be dangerous. What was Dayna thinking?

Eileen sniffled delicately into her embroidered lace hanky. "You have to do something, Luke."

"Dayna's old enough to make her own decisions." He privately thought Dayna was way off the mark when it came to this decision, but he would never tell his mother that. Eileen Callahan would dearly love a companion in browbeating her daughter-in-law. She had had that companion in her younger son, Steven, Dayna's husband. Steven had been killed in a car accident nearly a year ago, leaving Dayna with two small boys to raise. It was his opinion she was doing one hell of a job too.

"You have to go and bring Todd and Jesse back." Eileen reached for a little blue pill and slipped it into her mouth before taking a small sip of water. "My heart just can't stand the strain of them being out there in that . . . that . . . wilderness."

Her slip about bringing back the boys and not

Dayna didn't go unnoticed. Luke turned away from his mother and studied the garden. Discreet lighting revealed the slate path that wound through the lush garden. He wasn't too concerned about his mother's heart. She'd been crying wolf about her delicate condition for as long as he could remember. She used it when tears didn't get her her way.

"Dayna's taken the boys camping before," he said. "She won't let anything happen to them. She loves them."

"I love them too! They're all I have left of my poor Steven."

Luke's hands balled into fists as he shoved them into his pockets. *Her poor Steven!* His younger brother had reached sainthood in his mother's eyes long before his death. It was a real shame Steven had never reached his own lofty goals, much less come even close to sainthood. Steven had been a spoiled, self-centered, obnoxious little boy living in a man's world. A world their mother had created and cushioned for her baby, leaving her older son to fend for himself. Luke had done very well, without the help of his mother or their family name. He'd left Colorado immediately after graduating from college and had returned only infrequently over the years.

"You have to do something, Luke. They're the only grandchildren I have."

His mother's voice was as irritating as fingernails scratching a chalkboard. "What do you want me to do? Drive out there and haul them back home?"

"Yes." Eileen's voice had the authoritative ring

of a general's command now that her son appeared to be seeing things her way. "If you can't get married and give me some grandchildren to comfort my broken heart, the least you could do is take care of your nephews now that Steven is gone."

His brother's boys didn't need looking out for, Luke thought. They had their mother. Dayna had been raising those boys since the day they were born, without much help from Steven. His mother would never see it that way, though. Luke didn't give a rat's behind about family responsibility, but he did care about Todd and Jesse and their mother, Dayna. Sweet, beautiful Dayna who, after what Steven had put her through, would never look at another Callahan man as long as she lived.

Sighing heavily, he turned from the gardens and started to walk out of the room. "I'll be leaving at first light for Aces High."

ONE

Dayna Callahan looked at her younger son, Jesse, and smiled. He was soaked to his waist and having the time of his life. What was it about six-year-olds and water? She glanced over at her eight-year-old son, Todd, and her smile turned into a grin. Correction, what was it about boys and water?

The temperature was soaring into the eighties, and it was only midmorning. The clear, sparkling creek that rushed down the side of the mountain seemed frigid by comparison. There was still snow at some of the higher elevations in the Rockies at this time of the year. The creek apparently got its start in those heights.

"Jesse," she called, "are you looking for gold or are you playing with the water?" She watched, amused, as her son dumped the sieveful of rocks into the creek, creating a large splash that soaked Todd.

"Mom!" Todd cried. "Jesse splashed me." He

turned around and dumped his sieveful of rocks in front of his younger brother, returning the splashing gesture.

Jesse's little leg kicked at the water and ended up spraying her with the cold water. "Boys!" There wasn't any anger behind her word; the cold water felt wonderful, though shocking. For the past two days the boys had been diligently panning for gold without finding anything. They deserved a break today. Wasn't that what a vacation was all about, having a good time? Jesse and Todd deserved better than a "good time," they deserved a *great* time. She reached over, cupped a handful of water, and sprayed both of her sons.

The water fight was on. Within five minutes, sieves and pans were tossed up onto the bank and all three Callahans were soaked and laughing. Both Todd and Jesse had fallen in the creek and were dripping wet. She had enough water drenching her T-shirt to enter a wet T-shirt competition. She pulled the soaked shirt away from her skin and chuckled. She might enter the competition, but she would never win. Being generously endowed wasn't one of her better characteristics. A fact her husband had brought up numerous times in the last years of their marriage.

She shook her head to scatter any thoughts of her departed husband before they could form. She refused to think of Steven or the past. During this vacation she had vowed to enjoy her sons, the beauty of the mountains, and the quiet. There wasn't a soul within ten miles of this place to shatter their peace.

Dayna picked up a towel, dried her face and arms, then wrapped Jesse within its warmth. "That wasn't fair. Two against one are lousy odds."

"You're just mad because we won," Todd said. He picked up his towel and wiped the water from his smiling face.

Dayna would lose every water fight for the next ten years if it would keep that smile on Todd's face. For the past four years she had been worried about Todd. The boy took everything so seriously. It had only been in the past couple of months that she'd noticed a change in him. He'd been smiling more often, and the dimple in his right cheek had finally made a long overdue appearance. Her son was slowly coming back to her. It was sad that it had taken his father's death to achieve that goal. Steven had done more than just scar her emotionally; he had damaged his own sons with his indifference.

Todd looked like Steven with his dark hair and eyes, while Jesse had her golden hair and blue eyes. She loved both of her sons equally, but it was Todd who had suffered the most through the turbulent years. Jesse had been young enough to have been sheltered from the worst of it, while Todd had been old enough to see what was going on, but too young to understand. Damn Steven and damn his family for spoiling him so.

The only Callahan worth anything had passed away seven months earlier. Maxwell Callahan had been ninety-two when he took his last breath. He had spent the last seven years of his life in a nursing home with barely a visitor besides her and the boys. She'd started to visit Max soon after her marriage. Steven had encouraged the visits, even though he was always too busy to go. He had been hoping for a bigger inheritance from his grandfather. Dayna hadn't cared about that. She had looked forward to the visits with Max just to hear his stories. Max had been the head of the Callahan family and his adventures had been both daring and humorous. Over the years her sons had spent hour after hour listening to Max's stories and keeping company with the old man. Dayna hadn't been shocked to learn that Max had left something for his great-grandsons in his will. But she had been surprised by what.

One of Max's favorite stories was about how, in his younger days, he had won a ghost town in a poker game with an old prospector. The old prospector, presumably named One-eyed Pete, had had a pair of kings. Max had held a pair of aces. One-eyed Pete had handed over the deed to the land, then taken his mule and wandered off into the mountains, never to be heard of again. Max had renamed the town Aces High.

Dayna had thought the town was a wonderful inheritance and had started to plan their summer vacation accordingly. Being a junior high school history teacher, she tried to add the element of learning into every vacation she took with the boys. A ghost town in the Rockies was a perfect place for her sons to not only learn about mining gold and some history, but also to have a wonderful time.

"Come on, boys." She motioned to a blanket and picnic basket nestled near a group of pine trees. "I've packed us a midmorning snack." She had taken three steps toward the blanket when the silhouette of a man appeared at the top of the rise. With the sun directly behind him, she couldn't make out his features, only his size. She instinctively moved toward the boys and placed them behind her. Her chin rose a notch, her hands trembled, but her voice was steady as she called out, "This is private property."

"Do you think that would stop a criminal, Dayna?" the man answered.

"Uncle Luke!" Jesse and Todd shouted in unison as they scrambled around their mother.

Dayna frowned as Steven's brother smoothly made his way down the slippery slope. Luke Callahan did everything smoothly and gracefully. No matter what the situation, Luke always managed to adjust so naturally. What in the heck was the black sheep of the Callahan family doing two thousand miles from his home? If she were a betting woman, she would lay money that Eileen Callahan was behind his visit. Eileen had tried to talk her out of bringing the boys to Aces High. She hadn't listened then, and she wasn't about to listen now. Luke had made one very long trip for nothing.

Both of her sons met their uncle as he reached the creek bank and started to walk toward them.

Luke and Steven had the same dark hair and eyes, but there the similiarity ended. Luke had about three inches in height over his younger brother and had a harder, more physical appearance.

She watched as Luke greeted the boys, ruffled Todd's hair, then swung Jesse up into his arms. He didn't seem concerned about Jesse's soaked clothes. The boys had seen their uncle only twice in the past year—at Great-grandfather Max's funeral seven months earlier, and at their own father's funeral a few months before that. But neither was likely to forget their uncle. Luke Callahan was the kind of man you didn't forget once you met him. She knew that from experience.

There was something compelling about Luke Callahan. A friend of hers had once described Luke as having a male force field that pulled at every female's fantasy level. She wouldn't know about that. She no longer had any fantasies. They had all died years before. She had sworn off men, and even if she hadn't, Luke was a Callahan. She wouldn't touch another Callahan with a ten-foot pole!

He stopped a good four feet in front of her. "Hello, Dayna."

She inclined her head. "Luke." Her gaze skimmed him from top to bottom. A blinding white T-shirt clung to his chest and faded denim cradled his long legs. He had sturdy boots on his feet and dark sunglasses hid his eyes. The smile he had shown the boys had faded. She couldn't tell what he was thinking with those damn glasses on. "Aren't you a long way from home?"

"Heard you took the boys to see their inheritance."

Dayna felt the heat of his gaze travel the length of her body. She could just imagine what she looked like, but refused to show any embarrassment. The old tennis shoes she had on were perfect for wading in the creek, and her denim cutoffs might have seen better days, but they covered the necessary body parts. But she couldn't prevent her hand from reaching for her T-shirt and once again tugging it away from her chest. The drenched cotton immediately returned to its clinging position. She wasn't positive, but she would swear Luke's gaze focused on that wet shirt.

"I thought the boys would love to see Aces High," she said.

"We're panning for gold, Uncle Luke," Todd said.

"We only found zip so far," Jesse added importantly.

Luke pulled his gaze away from Dayna and lowered Jesse back to the ground. "Zip, you say?" He looked over to the assorted pans and sieves dotting the creek bank. "What are you using for bait?"

Todd and Jesse laughed. "You don't use bait, Uncle Luke," Todd said.

"Mom says you need something called luck," added Jesse.

"Your mom sounds like a very smart woman,

Jesse." Luke looked at her, and a small smile played at the corner of his mouth.

Dayna managed to return the smile, but it was strained. She didn't feel very smart. When it came to book smarts, she was at the head of the class. She had graduated from college with honors and a teaching degree. She loved teaching seventh and eighth graders American history. She could balance a checkbook, stick to a budget, and raise her two sons all on her own. But when it came to men, she was a total dunce. Anyone who had married Steven Callahan and then stuck by him for nearly eight years had to be moronic.

"We're about to have a snack," she said. "Would you care to join us?" What she really wanted to do was demand he get back into his car and leave them alone. This was supposed to be a peaceful, relaxing vacation, a private time for her sons and herself. For nine months out of every year she barely got any time alone with them. Between work, school, teachers' meetings, soccer practice, and life in general, they barely spent a couple hours each week together. She missed them terribly and tried every summer to spend as much time together as a family as they could. Luke Callahan might be the boys' uncle, but he wasn't family.

"Sure, I could use something to drink," he said. He followed her and the boys over to the plaid blanket spread out in the shade.

"Todd," Dayna said, "you and Uncle Luke can bring up the gallon of bottled water I wedged into the creek to keep it cool." She turned to Jesse. "You can help me set out the snacks." Without another glance at Luke, she sat on the blanket and reached for the basket. She heard Todd and Luke head for the creek. The low rumbling of Luke's voice as he talked to Todd slid down her back and caused her fingers to tremble.

How long had it been since she heard the murmuring of a man's voice? Months? Years? Steven had died nearly a year ago, but he hadn't been living at home for ten months before that. And even before then, it had been months since any male murmuring had entered her private life. For the past several years all Steven had known how to do was rant and criticize. She had taken it for the boys' sakes, until she just couldn't take it any longer. Then she had asked Steven to leave. Their divorce had been in process when he was killed.

She handed Jesse a box of cookies and took the plastic bowl filled with fresh fruit from the basket. A smile tugged at her mouth as Jesse ripped into the box of goodies. She selected a fat juicy plum for herself and set the bowl in the middle of the blanket.

Luke and Todd returned with the water. Luke poured and handed her and each boy a cup of cold water before sitting on the blanket. "It's as beautiful and quiet here as I remember," he said, looking around.

"You've been here before?" She didn't think any of the Callahans, besides Max, cared enough about the place to visit.

"Camped here a couple of times during the summer while I was in college."

"Did you see any bears?" asked Jesse.

"What about rattlesnakes?" added Todd.

Luke chuckled. "Sorry, boys." He swiped a cookie from the box Jesse was still holding. "Heard a coyote once."

"You did?" Jesse's eyes nearly bulged out of his small face.

Dayna glared at Luke. "I'm sure that was a real long time ago." What was he trying to do? Scare the boys into returning home?

"Your mom's right," Luke said. "It was a real long time ago. Most of the coyotes in this area are long since gone."

"What else did you see?" asked Todd.

"A few chipmunks, squirrels, and a porcupine once."

"Oh," Jesse mumbled. "We've seen all of them before."

"What about ghosts?" Todd asked.

Everyone turned in surprise to the boy. Dayna frowned at her son. "You know there is no such things as ghosts, Todd."

"You said this was a ghost town. So where's the ghost?"

Dayna gave a small chuckle. "A ghost town means there are no people living in the town, Todd. Not that there are ghosts roaming about. Aces High was once a small mining town, catering to the prospectors and such. When the gold ran out, the people left, abandoning the town to time and the elements."

"What about One-eyed Pete and his mule Freckles?" asked Todd.

Luke laughed. "I see someone was paying attention to my grandfather and his tales." He reached over and plucked an apple from the bowl of fruit. "Grandpop Max had a vivid imagination, Todd. There probably wasn't an old prospector named One-eyed Pete or a mule."

"So how did Great-grandfather win the town?" asked Jesse.

Dayna leaned back on her elbows and smiled. Luke was in for it now. He was daring to disagree with the tales the boys had heard all their lives. "Yes, tell us, Luke," she said. "If Max didn't win this town in a poker game, how did he get it?"

Luke stared across the blanket at her as he bit into the apple. "He could have just bought it."

"Not when he was twenty-two, Luke. If I remember the story correctly, Max Callahan didn't have two nickels to rub together when he was twenty-two. His fortune in railroads came when he was around thirty."

Luke raised one brow above the rim of his sunglasses. "Didn't realize you were so interested in the history of the Callahans."

"I'm always interested in history. My sons are Callahans, and they should know the history behind their name."

"Lord, yes," Luke said. "We wouldn't want

Todd or Jesse here to blacken such a distinguished name." He flashed both boys a wide grin.

Dayna had heard rumors about Luke and how after graduating from college he took off for the East Coast with nothing more than a suitcase full of clothes and a head full of ambition. Steven had denied those rumors and had told everyone who would listen that Luke had also taken with him a sizable inheritance of Callahan money and had used that as a springboard for the success he had made out of his life. Dayna wasn't exactly sure which story to believe, but Steven had always been a little too gleeful, a glint of malice shining in his eyes, every time he talked about Luke building his fortune on their father's money. It didn't matter to her how Luke had made his start, but she hoped the rumors were true. It would be nice to know that at least one Callahan had ambition in his soul, and she hoped her sons had inherited that from their uncle. Their father hadn't possessed one ounce of ambition and had avoided hard work and responsibilities as if they were plagues.

She sat up. "I don't think you would have to worry about Todd or Jesse blackening the Callahan name." As far as she was concerned, Steven had tainted the name beyond repair.

"I wasn't worried about that, Dayna." Luke seemed to be studying her closely. "I was only joking."

Todd and Jesse exchanged glances. "You want us to color the Callahan name?" Todd asked.

Luke chuckled and Dayna grinned. "I think that would be a wonderful idea, Todd," she said. "I do believe the Callahan name could use some color."

"I have to agree with your mom on that one," Luke said.

"What color should we paint it, Mom?" Jesse asked.

"When you get older you can paint it whatever color you want." She ruffled Jesse's golden hair. "Why don't you boys go on back to your search for fame and fortune? I have a couple of things I need to discuss with your uncle."

Todd and Jesse got up and dropped their empty paper cups in the bag Dayna had brought along for trash. "You're not leaving, are you, Uncle Luke?" Todd asked.

Dayna answered before Luke could say a word. "Don't worry, boys. Uncle Luke will say good-bye to you before he leaves."

Both adults stayed on the blanket, watching as the boys made their way to the creek. They were far enough away that they couldn't overhear Dayna and Luke, but not so far that the adults couldn't keep an eye on them.

Dayna took a deep breath and decided to get right to the point. "We aren't going back to Denver, Luke."

"Who asked you to?"

"You're about to." She kept her gaze on her sons. "I know Eileen called you and she's the reason you're here."

Luke leaned back on his elbows and stretched his legs out in front of him. "Positive about that one, are you?"

Her head jerked around and she stared at him. For one impossible instant she thought she had heard something totally unexpected in his voice. Something she couldn't put a name to. She must have been too long in the sun that morning to even contemplate the notion that Luke Callahan's voice had deepened with desire. "Are you denying that your mother called you?"

"She called."

Dayna wished he would take off those damn sunglasses so she could see his eyes. "And she asked you to drive out here and drag her poor grandsons back to civilization?"

"She asked."

She noticed that he didn't bother to correct her assumption that Eileen Callahan hadn't been concerned for her daughter-in-law. She knew Eileen would like nothing better than for a big hungry bear to come down off the mountain and have a Daynaburger for lunch. Everything would be so much simpler then. Eileen would be granted custody of her grandsons, and she could mold and shape them just as she had done with Steven. Dayna shuddered at the thought of her sons turning out like their father. Eileen wasn't an evil woman, just misguided in the ways of raising children.

"Todd and Jesse are having a wonderful time,

Luke." She didn't know why she was bothering to justify their vacation to her sons' uncle.

"I can see that they are." He glanced at the boys who were busily sloshing through water, panning for elusive gold nuggets.

"So go back to Denver and report to Eileen that they are fine and I won't let anything bad happen to my sons."

He turned back to her. "I don't report to my mother."

By the tight set of his jaw she could tell he didn't appreciate being referred to as Eileen's errand boy. "So what are you doing here?"

"Did you honestly think I would fly back home once I learned that you and the boys were camping at Aces High alone?"

"Why would you care what the boys and I do?" Luke had never interfered with her or her sons' lives before. He was a thoughtful and extravagant uncle who lived nearly two thousand miles away. He never forgot Christmas or a birthday, and he had offered financial help when Steven was killed. But he had never once meddled.

"I care what happens to my only nephews," he said. "And . . ." Through the dark-tinted glasses, his gaze locked with hers. "I happen to care about you very much."

TWO

Luke maneuvered the rented Jeep up the dirt road and applied the brakes at the top of the hill. He glanced down at the valley below and frowned. The dilapidated town of Aces High was spread out like a twisted reminder of the past. The collapsed remains of what had been the general store marked the beginning of the town. Dry-rotted lumber indicated the sites of a few other buildings. The Rock Gut Saloon was still standing and was in remarkably good shape. The same could be said for the stables at the end of town and the grand two-story structure that had been home for the richest man in town. The rest of the town was reverting slowly back to the dust and dirt it had been built on. It didn't take a genius to know what priorities the residents of Aces High had had.

The town was a sorrowful sight except for the electric blue and green of Dayna's tent and her bright red four-wheel drive Blazer parked nearby. She had strung a clothesline between the porch posts in front of the saloon, and three cheery yellow towels were drying in the late-afternoon breeze. What in the world had possessed her to bring the boys out here into the middle of nowhere? Granted, the town was now her sons', along with a substantial amount of money in trust for the boys' education, but wouldn't it have been better to treat the boys to a week at Disney World or something?

The sun was on its way down and the air was getting colder. Even in the middle of the summer, nights this high up in the Rockies were downright chilly. He had left Dayna and the boys to their panning before lunch and headed for Boulder. Since Dayna refused to listen to reason he had no choice but to move his schedule around. There was no way he was leaving Dayna and the boys alone out here.

It had taken him four hours in Boulder with a phone pressed against his ear to clear his schedule for the next week and a half. He'd spent another two hours shopping at a sporting goods store, a pharmacy, and a food store to pick up everything he would need for his unexpected vacation. The back of the Jeep was loaded with the supplies.

He had told Dayna he would be back, but he'd seen the skepticism in her blue eyes. Todd and Jesse had accepted his word, but Dayna had not. Who could blame her, though? From what little he knew about her marriage to his brother, a Callahan had been lying to her for years. Why would she believe another one? And why had it hurt so much that she hadn't?

Dayna had fascinated him from the first moment he had met her. It had been two days before she had married his brother, and he had just flown into Denver to attend the wedding. He had walked into his mother's house and literally bumped into her as she rounded a corner. He had been aware of the immediate attraction he felt for her, but he had squashed it the instant he learned she was soon to be his sister-in-law. Any woman who wanted to marry his brother, he had told himself, was not a woman he'd be interested in. Over the next few days he was in her company numerous times, and he slowly realized that Dayna wasn't the type of woman he'd pictured his brother marrying. The day after the wedding he flew back to Washington frustrated, edgy, and in an inexplicably foul mood. Over the years the foul mood returned every time he traveled to Denver to visit his mother and his brother and his family. Even the birth of his nephews had left an emptiness deep within his soul.

At first he'd written it off as a strange case of jealousy. His spoiled, pampered brother had found a wonderful woman to love him and give him children, while he was still searching for that elusive joy. Over the years he'd learned it wasn't that Steven had found someone to love him first. It was that he had found Dayna. Steven had found and married Dayna before Luke had even had a chance to know her. His younger brother had gotten the one woman he would have loved to call his own.

Now it was too late for him and Dayna. Steven was out of the picture and there didn't appear to be anyone else in Dayna's life, but it was still too late. Dayna would run fast and far if she had the slightest idea of how he felt about her. He knew it was hopeless to consider Dayna as anything more than his sister-in-law, but hope had a strange way of not listening to his head. The chance to spend the next week and a half in Dayna's company was just too good to pass up. It had all the elements of a fantasy and was just too damn tempting.

Dayna could like it or not, but he was staying with her and the boys. For the past nine years he had always put distance between them, not knowing how else to combat the attraction he felt for her. He was tired of staying away. Maybe once he learned who the real Dayna was, the attraction wouldn't be so strong.

Steven couldn't have made up all those negative and nasty things about his wife that Luke had heard over the years. If Steven was to be believed, Dayna was the most devious, whining, manipulative individual in the world. But Luke hadn't seen one thing since he'd known her that could justify Steven's complaints, but then again he'd never stayed in her company for more than a couple of hours at a time.

Muttering a curse, Luke released the brake and headed downhill. If the desire he'd felt that morning, seeing Dayna in a soaked T-shirt that clung to her breasts, was any indication, he was in for a week and a half of total frustration. Why was it that out of all the women he knew, Dayna was the one to fascinate him so? Was it a Freudian thing mixed up with sibling rivalry? He didn't know the answer. Hell, he wasn't even sure he wanted to know. But he was staying.

Like it or not, his mother was partly right. With Steven gone, Todd and Jesse needed a stable male influence in their lives, even if that influence lived more than halfway across the country. Dayna was an only child whose parents had died the year after her wedding. Luke and Steven's father had died more than ten years ago. Uncle Luke would just have to be around more for Todd and Jesse, which would make his feelings toward their mother all the more impossible to hide.

He slowed the Jeep as he neared the town and noticed the boys and their mother as they stepped off the wooden porch in front of the saloon. Both of his nephews waved and called his name. Dayna didn't look too pleased to see his return. He parked next to her Blazer and stepped out of the Jeep. He returned the boys' greeting and stretched the kinks out of his back. The road to Aces High was neither smooth nor paved. Making the journey twice in one day was enough to test any man.

"You came back!" Jesse shouted.

"We found lots of firewood, Uncle Luke," Todd said as he skidded to a halt in front of his uncle.

He noticed that all three of them had cleaned up

from the morning and had changed into jeans and sweatshirts. By bedtime, fire or no fire, they would all be wearing jackets and feeling the chill. He glanced at Dayna. "Mind if I borrow the boys to help me set up my tent?" He opened the Jeep's door wider, and both boys scrambled inside to scope out his recent purchases.

"So you're staying?" she asked.

"I told you I'd be back." He took a step closer to her to try to read her eyes. He couldn't.

"I don't put a lot of faith in a Callahan." Her voice was low so the boys wouldn't hear her comment.

It was one of the things he'd noticed about Dayna. She never degraded Steven's name in front of his sons. "I'm nothing like my brother, Dayna. Don't make that mistake."

She was silent, seeming to be studying his face. "I already figured that one out."

"How?"

"Steven wouldn't have come camping with his sons if someone had held a gun to his head." She gave him a brittle smile. "You may borrow the boys if you wish. I'll start dinner." She turned away without saying another word.

Luke watched her leave and felt the frustration rolling through his body. Dayna was still seeing Steven every time she looked at him.

◆━━━━━◆

Dayna hid her grin as Luke's tent collapsed for the second time. The small two-man tent should have taken him mere minutes to put up by himself. Instead, with the help of her sons it was going on half an hour and it still wasn't up. She could have warned Luke that having the boys help usually constituted more work, but she'd been curious as to how he would handle the boys. So far he was doing a masterful job at being patient, something Steven had never managed to do.

She hadn't been surprised when Luke had come back, but she was leery. Why would a man like Luke give up a week and a half of his time to camp in the middle of nowhere with his nephews and their mother? It made no sense to her. With Luke's money he should be soaking up some rays on a beach somewhere surrounded by women wearing string bikinis and inviting smiles. Not spending his time about to dine on hot dogs, baked beans, and canned macaroni and cheese, topped off with sparkling raspberry soda and gooey s'mores. She wouldn't trade camping with her sons for the romantic beach, but that was her preference. She just couldn't figure out Luke's choice.

Luke Callahan had always been a generous uncle. Over the years his job as president of the computer consulting firm he'd started had taken him to many foreign countries. A package for the boys always arrived the same time he returned home from one of his trips. The boys' gifts were either educational or just pure fun. The gifts he sent to his brother were usually for the house and she could tell very expensive.

Sometimes when she took the boys on vacation, they would find something they thought Uncle Luke would enjoy and she'd send it to him. Todd and Jesse also loved sending postcards to friends and family. Over the years Luke had probably received enough postcards to wallpaper his living room. He would always call the boys after their trips to hear all about what they did and to thank them for the cards. Steven couldn't have been bothered by the stories of his own sons' adventures, but Uncle Luke had cared. It was another difference between the two brothers that irked her. Why couldn't Steven have been more like Luke?

She opened the can of macaroni and cheese and dumped it into a pan to heat. Dinner was just about ready, and it appeared Luke's tent was going to stay up this time.

"We did it!" Jesse shouted.

Luke adjusted one of the poles and grinned at the boy. "So we did."

"What's next?" Todd asked.

"You guys can roll out my sleeping bag in the tent while I blow up the air mattress." Luke pulled a box containing a new mattress from the backseat of the Jeep.

"I have a foot pump if you want to use it," Dayna said.

"That would be great." He pulled the single mattress from the box.

Dayna turned the burner down under the pot and went in search of the pump. She found it buried in the back of the Blazer under an extra blanket and the suitcase containing all her clothes. She wiggled her way out of the vehicle and handed the pump to Luke. "It probably could be classed as an antique, but it still works."

"Thanks. I'm a little too old myself to go huffing and puffing."

"But you aren't an antique." She allowed her gaze to skim him from head to toe and added teasingly, "Yet." At thirty-seven Luke Callahan was the furthest thing from an old relic she could imagine, but for some strange reason she wanted to tease him. Steven couldn't stand to be teased, even if it was in jest. She wanted to see how Luke handled being kidded.

He grinned at her. "At least I still work."

Dayna gave him her first true smile since he'd shown up in Aces High. Luke could handle a simple joke. He would need that sense of humor if he planned on staying here with her two sons. Both Jesse and Todd had what Steven had classified as her "appalling" sense of humor. At times they also tended to push people past the edge of patience. To her way of thinking, having a sense of humor was imperative to raising kids. Luke just might make the remaining eleven days.

"Are you sure you'll have a company to go back to?" As far as she knew Luke didn't take vacations. If he did, she was positive Steven would have used that information in some way to torment her. Every achievement of Luke's had been just another excuse to complain.

"They can survive without me for a few days." He connected the hose to the mattress and started to pump with his foot.

Dayna went back to the stove and checked on dinner. The sun was just about behind the mountaintops. Within an hour they would all need their jackets and their flashlights. She glanced at his new tent and all the equipment he had obviously purchased on his trip into Boulder. "You weren't planning on staying more than a day or two when you left home, were you?"

"All I knew when I boarded the plane to Denver was there was some type of family emergency."

"Emergency?"

"My mother's word, not mine."

"So that's how she pulled you away from Washington." Dayna shook her head and stirred the bubbling beans. "Eileen was crying wolf again. One of these days she'll cry wolf and no one will come running." Dayna gave Luke a small smile. "Sorry about being the emergency. If I had known she would call you, I would have notified you first and saved you the trip. Eileen has a hard time realizing that I'm the mother of her precious grandsons and that I'm the one who calls the shots where they're concerned."

She held her breath and waited for his response. Steven would have pointed out, quite adamantly, that his mother was the only grandmother the boys had, and that she had a weak heart and the years were taking their toll on her. Eileen was his mother, he'd been fond of telling Dayna, and had every right to express her opinion. As his wife, Dayna had to learn to yield to his mother's wishes.

In the beginning, when the boys were small, she had tried to please both Steven and Eileen. She had missed her own mother terribly and was more than willing to try to fit Eileen into the empty spot in her life. But the more she gave, the more Eileen took. Eileen and Steven took, and took, and took, until Dayna didn't have anything left. Sometimes she thought there wouldn't ever be anything else again.

"Don't apologize for my mother, Dayna." Luke's foot increased its pace and the mattress grew fluffy. "She was right to be concerned for you and the boys being alone out here in the middle of nowhere, but you weren't an emergency. She should have told me what the problem was before I left Washington." The swishing of air being forced into the mattress accompanied his words. The mattress lost its fluffy, wrinkled look and became firmer. "All I kept thinking the whole way out here was something happened to you or the boys."

Dayna glanced at the mattress. It appeared ready to burst at its seams. "You can stop pumping now." She noticed that he didn't totally disagree with his mother. It was an improvement over Steven's obsessive devotion to the woman, but it still grated on her nerves.

She was at a loss, however, on how to respond to

his statement about worrying about her and the boys. It was awfully sweet of him to be so concerned, but totally unnecessary. Over the years she'd learned she didn't need someone hovering about, concerned with her or the boys. She hadn't needed Steven for nearly a year before his death, and she surely didn't need someone now.

She gave the pot one last stir. "Dinner's ready." She glanced at the boys as they came out of Luke's tent. "Todd, you get out the plates and silverware. Jesse, why don't you and Uncle Luke go down to the creek and haul up that six-pack of soda I have chilling."

Luke barely had time to slip the mattress into his tent before Jesse grabbed his hand and tugged him in the direction of the creek. By the time they returned carrying a dripping six-pack, dinner was served.

Holding their plates carefully, the boys sat in their folding chairs near the pile of kindling they'd light later. It was one of the boys favorite things to do. After dinner they would clean up and light a fire and roast marshmallows while their mother told tales of old prospectors, long forgotten towns, and the proud people who had once called these mountains their home, the Ute Indians.

She glanced up at Luke as he held out his plate. The same boyish smile Jesse had worn a moment earlier was now on his face. Luke even had the same dimple in his right cheek. She was in trouble now. She couldn't refuse Jesse a single thing when he flashed that dimple. How was she going to stand firm against Luke and the Callahan name when he flaunted such an intriguing characteristic?

Luke's face was all rough planes and sharp angles, and she would have sworn there was nothing soft about him. Now she wasn't so sure. Not only was there a dimple playing peekaboo with the hard bracket of his mouth, but in the late-day sunlight his hair looked temptingly soft, and a wayward curl kept falling over his forehead, begging to be brushed back. Her fingers fairly itched to do just that. She wished he would ditch the sunglasses so she could see his eyes. The eyes were supposed to be the window of the soul. And for some unexplained reason, she wanted to see Luke's soul.

She plopped a couple of spoonfuls of macaroni and cheese and baked beans on his plate. "I'm sure this isn't what you are used to eating, but it's filling." She placed a hot dog in a roll and added it to his plate.

"Smells delicious." He took a fork and a cold soda from the back tailgate and joined the boys. The green-striped folding chair was one of his new purchases, and the price tag dangled to the ground when he sat down.

Dayna started to fill a plate for herself. She had made extra food tonight for Luke, but her supplies wouldn't last as long as she had figured if she was feeding an additional adult. It meant a trip into Meeker Park, the nearest town with a food store, within the next couple of days. "Does everyone have everything before I sit down?" she asked. It had been her experience that as soon as she sat down, one of the boys would need something.

"Everyone's fine, Dayna," Luke said. "Sit down and eat before your dinner gets cold."

She balanced her plate in one hand and reached for a soda and fork with the other. Joining them, she slowly sank into her chair. No sooner had she popped the top of her soda when Jesse said, "Mom, I forgot to get my soda."

She gave a silent groan and was about to stand back up when Luke's voice stopped her. "Since you forgot the soda, Jesse, I suggest you go get it."

Jesse looked at his uncle in confusion. "But Mom gets us everything."

"Since your mom cooked your meal and just asked if you had everything, I think it's only fair that you get your own soda."

Dayna wasn't sure what surprised her more. That Jesse didn't argue further and got up to retrieve his own drink, or that Luke had insisted that Jesse do it himself. Steven wouldn't have reached across the table for the salt if she was around. She'd once caught him telling the boys that that was why God had made females. So babies could be born and so men wouldn't go hungry. She also remembered the terrible fight they had had that night over his philosophy and the lessons he was teaching their sons. Their marriage had already been heading downhill faster than an avalanche, but Steven had a way of forcing that avalanche to go faster. She tried to show the boys how wrong their father had been, but every time they visited their grandmother, she fussed around them so much, Dayna was amazed Eileen allowed them to visit the bathroom alone. Eileen's behavior only reinforced everything Steven had told the boys. She had expected the same from Luke, but she was obviously wrong.

The meal passed in remarkable tranquillity as the boys told their uncle about their day and Todd proudly showed Luke the hunk of fool's gold he had found in the creek.

THREE

Dayna watched as her sleepy-eyed sons entered the tent and zipped the flap behind them. It was one of the cardinal rules of camping; if you're not going in or out of the tent, zip the flap. Dayna considered herself self-reliant and a semicourageous woman of the nineties. Finding a slithering snake in their tent, though, would have pushed her beyond her capabilities. She hated insects, rodents, and snakes. It was a strange and bothersome character flaw considering she loved camping and being outdoors.

She glanced at Luke. He looked ready to fall asleep in his chair. His jean-clad legs were stretched out in front of him, toward the dancing flames. He had pulled on a gray sweatshirt advertising the Smithsonian Institution, but he hadn't added a jacket. He was slouched deep into the chair and appeared not to have a care in the world.

What cares could he possibly have? she asked

herself. The man owned a prestigious computer consulting firm. The list of his clients read like a who's who in Washington. Computers were the wave of the future, and apparently every civil servant in the hallowed halls of the government wanted to surf the Net. They all needed systems to talk to one another, to converse with their constituents back home, and to give them access to the Super Highway. Luke's firm saw to it that every criterion was met and enhanced. The way the politicians came and went on Capitol Hill, Dayna figured Luke had one of the securest jobs in the Beltway.

As for his personal life she knew zip. Steven always claimed that Luke was against marriage, against kids, and opposed any act of commitment. Of course, Steven had claimed a lot of things during their marriage, and most were lies. With Luke, however, she wasn't too sure. In all his trips home, he had never once had a female companion. She had never even heard his name linked to a woman's. A couple of times she had wondered which way Luke Callahan swung, but instinct had given her the answer. Luke was definitely a ladies' man, but for some reason he kept his personal life personal. Not that she could blame him.

If he had ever brought a woman during one of his rare visits, Eileen would have been calling in wedding consultants and ordering the flowers. Nothing would have given her more pleasure than seeing Luke married, living nearby, and presenting her with a few more grandchildren to spoil.

An interesting thought drifted through Dayna's mind. Maybe if Luke did get married, it would take some of the pressure off her and the boys. Eileen would have someone else to try to control.

She stretched out her feet toward the fire and slouched down in her chair. She had been dreading the time when the boys disappeared into the tent for the night, leaving her alone with Luke. But maybe if she dug a little bit, she could hand Eileen a nice juicy bone of a pending new daughter-in-law, thereby diverting Eileen's intense interest away from her and the boys. Eileen could be a wonderful woman if she only learned to butt out occasionally.

"So, how's the business going?" she asked Luke. It seemed like a good place to start.

Luke didn't move a muscle, but she had the impression all of his attention was focused on her. "We posted an eighteen percent increase in profits last year."

"That's great." Okay, she had just proven how successful the man was. Now for the more personal stuff. "Eileen told me that you bought a house last year."

This time his head turned in her direction. "Yes, I did."

"What type? One of those nice Federal homes in the Georgetown section?" It seemed like the type of house a well-off businessman would buy. A nice investment in the most prominent neighborhood in the District of Columbia.

"No. I purchased an old stone home on the out-skirts of Manassas."

"That's Bull Run!" She wasn't a history teacher for nothing. She knew her Civil War. Hell, in her younger days she'd read everything she could about that period. She'd even backpacked through the area during a break in college. "How old is the house?"

"Built somewhere around eighteen thirty. I don't have the actual record. Most records were destroyed in the war."

He was living in a house whose walls had heard and seen the horrors of that war! "Any proof or even stories about the house being part of the war?"

Luke shifted in his chair and grinned at her. "I found some indications that the house was used as a headquarters during one of the major battles."

Her jaw dropped open and she gaped for a full minute before her brain kicked back in. "What bat-tle and who used it?" she demanded.

"From what I've discovered so far, it appears to have been a headquarters for Pierre Beauregard dur-ing the first battle of Bull Run." His grin widened. "He was a Confederate general, in case you were wondering."

"I knew who he was!" This time it took more than a minute to get her brain back in gear. Luke was living in a bloody museum! "Why hasn't the state or federal government purchased the house for its historical value?"

"No solid proof that it was used as a headquarters. Without something concrete it's just another house on the historical register."

"A house that you own."

"Correct." He gave her an amused glance. "Maybe next time you want a vacation, instead of panning for gold, you and the boys could come out and give me a hand searching for the proof, or at least help me to select some furniture. I'm trying to redo the entire house in the Civil War time period, but with modern conveniences."

She was tempted to pack up the Blazer and head for Virginia that very minute. Why hadn't Eileen told her that Luke had purchased a slice of history? If she wasn't careful, he was going to notice she was drooling. "We wouldn't cramp your style or the house if we popped in for a visit?"

"It has four bedrooms, three of which aren't in use. You and the boys are more than welcome to come anytime." He went back to slouching in the chair and staring at the fire. After a minute he added, "There's plenty for the boys to see and do. D.C. is right there, and then there's the battlefields. There's also Williamsburg, Yorktown, and Jamestown toward the bottom of Virginia, along with Virginia Beach. And to the west there's the Blue Ridge Mountains and the Shenandoah Valley."

Dayna had to laugh. Luke was sounding like a travel agent. "Stop it, please." She shook her head. "We'll come. We'll come." The devil himself couldn't keep her away from such a tempting treat.

"You will?"

Why did he sound so skeptical? "I said we'll come. Why wouldn't we?" If he hadn't invited them, she might have gotten down on her hands and knees and begged.

"You never came before."

"We were never invited before." She had tried to weasel an invitation years earlier to visit Washington, but Steven had told her not to pressure his brother. If Luke had wanted a bunch of kids and a woman underfoot, Steven had said, he would have married and had some of his own.

Luke looked at her. "I issued an invitation at least twice a year since Todd was born. Steven always had a ready excuse as to why you all couldn't come. I stopped asking about two years ago."

Dayna shook her head. "I'm sorry, Luke. I never knew about the invitations, or the boys and I would have come. Steven wasn't one for taking a vacation with his family." It was the kindest way of phrasing what kind of jerk Luke had had for a brother. She knew Luke and Steven had never been close, but they still had been brothers. She could feel Luke's gaze on her and prayed the darkness hid the flush staining her cheeks.

"Steven wasn't one for doing much of anything with his family, was he?"

She debated how to answer that. She always believed in telling the truth, but now she had to wrestle with the added problem of not speaking ill of the dead. Steven was no longer alive to defend his actions, even if there wasn't an excuse that could have defended his terrible indifference toward his family.

"You can tell me the truth, Dayna. I know what kind of man my brother was."

"Really?" Luke lived far away and had spent an average of four days a year in the company of his brother. How well could he have known what type of man Steven had become?

"Let's see," he said. "Spoiled, selfish, blamed everyone else for his own mistakes, always searching for that elusive quick buck . . ."

"Okay, so you do have a general idea of what Steven was like." Luke didn't know everything, though, she thought. Nobody knew everything, at least she prayed they didn't. Steven hadn't been physically abusive, but he had been mentally and emotionally abusive. No matter what she did, it had never been good enough for Steven. For years she had blamed herself and wondered what she had been doing wrong. By the time Todd entered school, she'd known their marriage was over. It had taken her another year before she got up the courage to tell Steven.

"I never could figure out what you saw in him, why you married him."

"I met Steven on a double date in my last year at the University of Denver. I was going out with a guy I'd had a few dates with and my roommate was dating Steven. By the end of the night, both my date and my roommate were out of the picture."

"Didn't that make for an awkward evening?"

"Not really. Carl, my date, didn't seem too broken up with the idea and my roommate didn't mind because she was only going out with Steven to make her ex-boyfriend jealous. Steven wined and dined me, swept me off my feet. Our wedding was two weeks after I graduated."

She didn't go into how gorgeous Steven had been or how the Callahan name was equivalent to God in Denver. Luke knew that. But the main factor that had convinced her to marry Steven was she had really, honestly been in love with him. Problem was, Steven had been in love with only himself. Her love for Steven had taken a lot of bruising before it died. It would take a minor miracle before she risked her heart again.

"I would guess," Luke said, "that whirlwind courtships aren't your favorite thing right about now."

She chuckled. "Courtships of any variety aren't my favorite thing."

"You're not interested in forming another relationship with a man?"

"I'm sorry, Luke, but you missed the point. I might have lived with your brother, but we didn't have a relationship, much less a marriage. It takes two people to build and sustain a marriage, and what we had was me banging my head against a wall and Steven standing aloft and arrogant on the other side."

"So why did you stay married to him for all those years?"

Dayna was silent for a long time as she studied the flames, watching them dance and consume the wood Luke kept adding. It was still hard to look back at the past years. It was harder still to tell someone like Luke what a fool she had been. He didn't seem like a guy who suffered fools gladly.

"In the beginning," she said, "I really didn't know what to expect out of marriage. I don't think anyone does. It's kind of like free-falling off a cliff. Some couples are lucky enough to have their parachute work and they descend gracefully, while others need the reserve chute to catch them." She looked over at Luke and managed a small smile and a shrug. "Others like Steven and me just keep falling until we go splat."

"Eight years is an awfully long time to be free-falling, Dayna."

"At first, I didn't realize we were free-falling. Besides, it was seven years, not eight."

"Seven?"

She studied Luke's face in the soft glow of their campfire. He looked confused. For the first time she wondered if he didn't know that she and Steven had been separated for ten months before his car accident. "Steven and I were in the process of getting a divorce at the time of his death. He'd moved out nearly a year earlier."

"No one told me. Why didn't you mention it when I flew in for the funeral?"

"Aside from the fact that I figured you knew, when would I have said anything? During the church service or at the funeral home? How about over the catered reception your mother had at her home after the burial?"

"You're right, but it still doesn't explain why Steven never mentioned it to me. I talked to him a couple of weeks before he was killed, and he left me with the distinct impression that everything was just fine on the home front. He said something about Todd having a great checkup at the dentist and how Jesse had learned to ride the two-wheeler I had sent him for Christmas, without the training wheels."

"Steven told you those things?" She didn't know what surprised her more—that Steven had given Luke the impression they were still together, or that her late husband had actually mentioned the boys. Steven hadn't been big on parental concern. In fact, as long as the boys didn't require any of his time or money he was perfectly content. The problem with children was they required an abundance of both.

Luke glanced over at the tent. The boys had long ago shut off their flashlights and settled down for the night. "My brother didn't care about his sons too much, did he?"

"Let's put it this way." She kept her voice low. "He wouldn't know Todd's dentist's name or what kind of checkup he'd had. He probably never even knew the boys went to the dentist. Steven also never once saw Jesse ride the bike you sent him."

"My brother wouldn't have won any father-of-the-year awards, would he?"

"As far as Steven was concerned, he did his duty by getting me pregnant. The rest was up to me."

His gaze seemed to linger on her face. "He wouldn't have won any husband-of-the-year awards either, would he, Dayna?"

She felt a flush sweep up her face and prayed the darkness hid the evidence of her embarrassment. "Drop it, Luke. He's gone, and it's all in the past now."

"Is it?"

"Is it what?"

"In your past. You said you don't date, so I have to assume there's still a lot of unresolved issues concerning your marriage."

"You know what they say when you assume something, Luke." She didn't like to be analyzed, and the last person in the world she would tell about the problems she had with Steven was his brother. They were humiliating enough without actually verbalizing them.

"Since Steven died about eleven months ago," Luke said, "and since you were separated for almost a year before that, I guess it's safe to *assume* another man wasn't the reason behind the breakup?"

She nearly laughed. *Another man!* If she was willing to suffer humiliation at the hands of another man, which she was not, when would she find the time? Contrary to some current public opinions, being a teacher was a demanding, unending, and thankless job. She spent her days trying to teach American history to a bunch of twelve- and thirteen-year-olds whose hormones were ricocheting off the classroom walls. When she got home at night, she barely had the energy to take care of her sons, let alone the mountain of chores awaiting her.

Her life hadn't been much different with Steven. He wouldn't have known one end of a vacuum cleaner from the other. He had never so much as made a slice of toast, let alone dinner. She had even mowed the lawn and taken out the trash. By bedtime she'd been ready to drop into a deep sleep, but often had to listen to her husband's complaints about her inability to excite him sexually.

Steven had been her first and only lover. In the beginning of their marriage she had made up for her inexperience with enthusiasm and had been satisfied with the results. She'd thought Steven had been too. When he'd started to complain, after Jesse's birth, she had believed him and had tried numerous ways to become more appealing. The birth of their sons had taken a toll on her body, but she had thought it was a small price to pay for the love they brought into her life. Steven obviously thought differently. So she did more stomach crunches than Jane Fonda, ate like a bird, and tried to become more inventive behind closed doors. She maxed out her credit card with see-through negligees, French-cut panties, satin sheets, and seductive perfume. Nothing worked. Steven's complaints just grew as their sex life diminished.

"No, Luke," she said, "there wasn't another man." The painful memories caused a spurt of resentment. "But there were plenty of women. Your brother was a real ladies' man." Toward the end of their marriage she had suspected Steven had been fooling around. When she'd decided that no husband was better than the one she had and told him to leave, he had laughed and confessed to having affairs with other women as far back as two months after their wedding. His cruel parting comments had cut deeper than she would have imagined. The scars might not be visible to the human eye, but they were there.

"Steven fooled around?"

Dayna almost laughed at Luke's incredulous tone of voice. Anyone hearing him would think Steven had to have been crazy to choose another woman over her. "Steven fooled around a lot, Luke. He referred to it as 'The Old Callahan Charm.'"

His frown was clearly visible by the glow of the fire. "Not all Callahans have that charming quality, Dayna."

"No?" Luke looked like he could get any woman he wanted. And judging from the stories she'd heard, his father had been the same. Eileen Callahan had had her hands full with her husband, the famous Joseph Callahan, and his wandering eye. From all accounts, his eyes weren't the only thing that had wandered. Joseph had died of a heart attack at age forty-eight in the bed of his twenty-one-year-old mistress. And if Maxwell's stories could be believed, not only had he gone through five different wives, but it would have taken a football stadium to hold all his mistresses. Dayna had decided that the only stick you could measure a Callahan by was the one bulging in his pants.

"I'm not like my father and brother." Luke's answer was growled across the darkness.

Dayna backed off the obviously touchy subject. Luke didn't like to be lumped together with the rest of the Callahan men. She couldn't blame him. The nicest one in the group had been Max, and he had been ninety-two, toothless, and totally harmless. But in his younger days she was positive he'd given plenty of women nothing but trouble and heartache.

With a heavy sigh she tossed a twig into the fire. "Tell me more about your home, Luke. It sounds fascinating . . ."

An hour later, Luke watched the play of Dayna's flashlight inside her tent. He could tell exactly what she had been doing since she'd entered the tent two minutes earlier. First she had checked on the boys. Now she was changing into some type of sleeping outfit. Only her intriguing silhouette could be seen against the nylon of the tent. That innocent silhouette was enough to speed up his heart rate and to detour all his blood to one sensitive location. He continued to watch as she slipped into her sleeping bag and shut off the flashlight. Darkness filled the tent and his thoughts.

Steven had viciously and knowingly lied to him all these years. Steven had painted Dayna as a whining shrew and one of the major causes of all his problems. When Luke had visited he'd known all was not well in the marriage. He'd seen it in the sadness lurking in Dayna's eyes and the exhaustion pulling at her face. Being married to Steven had given her plenty of cause to be a whining shrew, but he doubted if she ever was one. He thought of her as a loving and caring mother. Anyone could see how much she loved her sons. He remembered Steven telling him once that he wanted a daughter, but Dayna wouldn't hear of it. Luke wondered now if she really didn't want any more children, or if it was just that she was too tired from raising the boys by herself.

He turned away from the tent and contemplated the fire. There was something else, besides the obviously bad marriage, that was keeping Dayna from dating. A relationship between a man and a woman was the most natural thing in the world. A beautiful, intelligent, and loving woman like Dayna should have a string of men following her. He was glad there wasn't, but it seemed so unnatural to him. Something was holding Dayna back. He had heard it in her voice, and it had caused fear to snake its way through him.

What had transpired between his brother and Dayna behind closed doors? He knew it was none of his business, but he was going to make it his business. Dayna was just too damn important to him not to.

He smiled as he nudged a log farther into the

flames with the tip of his boot. Dayna had been fascinated by his description of his house. She and the boys would be coming out for a visit real soon. He could tell she was hooked. It was just one of the many things they had in common, their love of history.

Now if only he didn't scare her away by doing something real stupid, like kissing her. The thought of kissing Dayna had always played on the outer fringes of his mind, but now it was front and foremost. Being this close to her for eleven days was going to play more than havoc on his control. How was he supposed to treat her like a member of his family when all he wanted to do was drag her to the ground and satisfy nine years of hunger?

With a muffled curse, he kicked the log, sending a shower of sparks flying up into the night air. The last thing Dayna needed was to be dragged to the ground. She had had a hard marriage and was struggling now to raise two boys on her own. He was a mature man who should be able to control whatever desire he had for her and act the part of the perfect uncle. Uncles did not go around kissing their late brother's wives, no matter how much they wanted to.

FOUR

Dayna plastered a sickly smile onto her face and continued onward and upward, following the testosterone-driven males hiking in front of her. Her career choice of sitting behind a desk or standing in front of a blackboard all day had finally taken its toll. For the first time, she could no longer keep up with her sons. Then again, this was the first time she hadn't been setting the pace. This afternoon's grueling hike up the side of Bald Mountain hadn't been her idea. This was supposed to be a relaxing vacation, which meant doing nothing more strenuous than breathing in fresh, clean mountain air. No, climbing Bald Mountain had been their illustrious tour guide's idea, dear, sweet, *soon-to-be-dead* Uncle Luke.

The man was relentless in his pursuit of gaining the best vantage point for showing his nephews the eagles that claimed this mountain range as their home. Granted, she had been all for the adventure when they had set out over two hours earlier. Now, she wanted nothing more than to soak her aching toes in some cool stream and take a long nap. Both Todd and Jesse were still filled with energy and were contentedly bouncing along beside Luke, chattering up a storm. If for one moment she thought her sons needed a break, she would demand a halt to this torture, but both of them looked ready to conquer Mt. Everest. There was no way she was admitting she needed a rest before her six-year-old son.

There was only one person to blame for her screaming thighs, and his name was Luke Callahan. The man was going to pay, and pay dearly, for this. She didn't know when, and she didn't know how, but pay he would. No eagle was worth this. The bird would have to be sprouting six wings and be as bald as a baby's behind to be worth the agony her legs were in.

The breathtaking scenery had ceased to impress her a mile back. Mother Nature was reduced to a hazy blur in her peripheral vision. Her entire concentration was focused on placing one foot in front of the other and keeping some sort of smile on her face. She squinted at the three males a good nine yards in front of her and corrected herself. Part of her brain was concentrating on something else—the enticing back view of her brother-in-law. No, Luke was no longer her brother-in-law. He was still her sons' uncle, but he wasn't related to her. And her non-relative had one very fine looking rear.

For years she could not figure out why women talked about or scoped out men's backsides. When some of the other female teachers whispered about Mr. Tracy, the boys' gym teacher, and his buns of steel, she had been at a total loss. She had chalked it up to just one more boat of life she had missed while it was docking. Now, she wasn't so sure. Luke's bottom definitely had a certain appeal.

She was torn between fantasies. The vision of wringing Luke's neck and tossing him off the top of Bald Mountain for coming up with this harebrained bird-watching expedition was a good one. But then again, if she concentrated really hard, she might conjure up a pretty accurate picture of what Luke looked like beneath the faded denim that clung to his hips and legs. Decisions, decisions!

"Hey, we're almost there!" Todd shouted.

Dayna followed the arch of her son's hand and silently groaned. The rocky lookout that Luke had promised them loomed about two hundred yards in front of them. The actual yardage wasn't bad. It was the damn forty-five degree slope a person would have to climb to reach the lookout that had her sweating. Nix the fantasies about Luke's buns of steel, the man was going to die.

"How are you holding up back there, Dayna?" Luke asked as he turned around and glanced at her.

"Just peachy." She was beginning to hate those sunglasses he always wore. She would have bet one of the bottles of water jammed into their backpack that there had been laughter in his voice. It didn't improve her mood knowing that Luke was carrying the heavy pack while she and the boys carried nothing more strenuous than sturdy walking sticks and binoculars strung around their necks.

Luke had no right to find humor in her discomfort. So she was a little out of shape. Scaling Pikes Peak wasn't on her aerobic videotape at home. The day Luke Callahan delivered two eight-and-a-half-pound babies was the day he could pass judgment on the shape she was in.

She forced herself to give him a winning smile, even as she felt the strain of her facial muscles clear down to her calves. "Are we here already?"

One corner of his mouth twitched. "I told you it was only a short hike."

Jesse left Luke's side and ran back to his mother. "Gee, Mom, your face is all red."

Dayna refused to look at Luke. "It's the sun, sweetie. I forgot to put on sunblock before we left." She placed her hand on Jesse's shoulder and moved him in the direction of the lookout. Now that she had a two-minute breather, there was a possibility—a slim possibility—that she might make it after all. "Let's go see those eagles Uncle Luke promised us."

Ten minutes and a pint of cool spring water later, Dayna felt semihuman. The urge to push Luke over the edge was fading as the thunderous pounding of her heart slowed. Jesse and Todd sat on a large boulder a couple of feet in front of her, eagerly scanning the brilliant blue sky in search of eagles. Luke was sipping his bottle of water and scanning the rocky lookout. For what, she didn't know, nor was she going to ask. Instinct told her she wouldn't like his answer.

Didn't snakes like to slither out onto nice warm rocks to sun themselves? That was one of the reasons she and her sons never strayed from the marked paths when they camped in the national parks. Most forest creatures feared humans, so they stayed away from the well-traveled paths, and Dayna had always felt safe on those trails. Camping at the Aces High was a risk, but she figured with all the noise the boys made, any snake worth his rattler would be halfway to New Mexico within five minutes of their arrival. So far that logic had proved correct. She hadn't seen so much as a dried-up old skin the four days they had been there. Now the mighty hiker had taken them into unknown territory.

"Jesse, Todd, would you like some more water?" Her voice was unusually and purposely loud, but she wanted to make their presence known to all of God's creatures.

Both boys jumped, and Luke chuckled. "Mom," Todd said as he jokingly rubbed his ears, "we're right in front of you."

She took the first-aid kit from the pack and slammed it onto a rock. "Sorry." She had the grace to flush. "Are you still thirsty?"

"No," answered Todd as he lifted his binoculars to the sky again.

"No thanks, Mom." Jesse quickly followed his

brother's lead and brought his own pair of binoculars back up to his eyes.

Dayna nervously glanced around at the surrounding rocks as Luke lowered himself onto the same boulder where she had parked her weary body.

"Relax," he whispered. "Any snake with half a brain is all the way to the Colorado River by now."

"It's the ones without half a brain I'm worried about."

Luke replaced the plastic top on his water bottle and set it aside. Stretching his legs out in front of him, he studied the sky. "Never knew you had a thing about snakes."

"Being a single parent turned me into a worrywart." She followed his gaze and searched the heavens for any signs of a bird.

"Must be difficult raising the boys on your own."

She gave a halfhearted shrug but didn't comment. Hard didn't begin to describe it, but she wouldn't trade places with anyone. She loved Jesse and Todd with everything she had, and then some. The boys were whispering and watching the sky, not paying the slightest attention to her or Luke. Now seemed like a perfectly good time to bring up a subject long overdue. "There's something I need to talk to you about."

He turned his head toward her and raised one dark brow. "So talk."

"It's kind of personal." She swallowed hard and fidgeted with the first-aid kit before placing it back into the pack.

"Now I'm curious."

"I should have told you months ago, but I didn't know how."

"Curiouser and curiouser."

She bit her bottom lip and wondered how to begin. Luke extended one finger and pulled the lip out from beneath her teeth. A strange fiery sensation erupted where he touched her. She tried to see his eyes, wondering if he felt the heat, but she could only see the reflection of the sun bouncing off the dark lenses.

"Take a deep breath and say it, Dayna." His finger lingered on her lip for longer than necessary before he lowered his hand.

"I've made you guardian of Todd and Jesse in case anything happens to me." There it was out. She knew she shouldn't have named him guardian without speaking to him first. But after Steven had died she'd begun to worry what would happen to the boys if something happened to her. Eileen was a good person deep down inside, but she was a terrible mother. Well, Luke hadn't turned out half bad, so she had some redeeming motherly qualities, but Dayna still didn't want Eileen raising her sons. Their uncle Luke was her only option. From everything she had seen and heard about him, he was a good, hardworking, decent man. She knew he didn't want children or the responsibility of them, but she had no other choice.

She watched as every ounce of color drained from his face and knew she had made a major mistake. Maybe her friend Carol wouldn't mind being named guardian. After all, what were two more kids when she already had four of her own?

"Are you ill?" Luke asked hoarsely. He grasped her shoulders, his fingers digging in.

"No." She shook her head. This wasn't the reaction she had been expecting. Maybe Luke thought she was dying. "I'm perfectly healthy."

"You're not sick?" His fingers loosened their grip, and color slowly returned to his face.

"No, I'm fine." She gave him a smile that she hoped was full of health. "I needed to name someone as guardian just in case, so I picked you." She glanced at her sons, who were still whispering and joking around. "I'm sorry for scaring you like that. I'll change my will as soon as we get back to Denver."

"Change it? Why?"

"Why?" She gave a low chuckle. "I saw your panic, Luke." She patted his hand. "Don't worry, I won't force parenthood on you. Steven told me how adverse you were to becoming a parent. I should have listened."

"Steven told you that?"

"On more than one occasion. He told me you were antimarriage, antikids, and anticommitment."

"And you believed him?"

"Well, you haven't married, and Eileen would have told me if there were any other grandchildren dotting the country. So, I figured there might have been an ounce of truth in Steven's words."

Luke sighed and turned away.

He seemed to be searching the heavens for eagles, but she had a feeling he was looking for something to say. She presumed he was trying to figure out the nicest way to ask her to remove his name as guardian without sounding too uncaring. She never should have named him as guardian without talking it over with him first. If a man didn't want the responsibility of raising his nephews, he shouldn't be forced into it.

She reached out and touched his arm. "It's okay, Luke. I understand."

"What do you understand, Dayna?"

At the harshness in his voice, her teeth again sank into her lower lip. Luke sounded more upset with her than with the prospect of becoming her sons' guardian. "I know you like the boys, Luke. But liking them and having them dropped on your doorstep are two different things. I shouldn't have named you without discussing it with you first. But after Steven died I began to experience what I call 'single parent' attacks."

"What are single parent attacks?"

"Crazy stuff." Her smile was self-mocking. "You know, visions of a meteor falling from the sky and dropping on my head. The Oliver Twist story with Jesse and Todd as the lead characters begging for more gruel. Dreams of your mother molding the boys into perfect little replicas of Steven." She shrugged. "I told you, crazy stuff."

"Doesn't sound too crazy to me. Sounds more

like a mother who loves her sons very much." He reached over and gently squeezed her hand. "I'll be honored to be named Todd and Jesse's guardian, on one condition."

"What's that?" Thank God! She didn't know what she would have done if he had refused. Carol might be her best friend, but being someone's friend was a lot different than raising their kids.

Strong masculine fingers intertwined with her smaller ones. "Try not to let any meteors fall on your head."

She couldn't stop the laughter that bubbled up from her throat. It was like a giant weight had been lifted from her shoulders. "I'll try really hard."

He smiled. "You should do that more often."

"What?" She was fascinated by the curve of his mouth. Since when had Luke developed such an enticing mouth? Hell, since when had she started noticing men's mouths, for cripes sake? And why had this latest development started with Luke of all people?

He leaned in closer and whispered, "Laugh."

Dayna's gaze shot up to his, only to encounter dark glasses. There it was again, that deepening of his voice that sent shivers of need down her spine. How could he make one word sound so sexy?

She shook her head at the absurdity of it all. Luke Callahan might be considered sexy as sin by some women, but she knew to stay away. He was a Callahan, cut from the same mold as Steven, their cheating father, and even lovable, yet insatiable Max.

"Hey, Mom, look!" Jesse cried as he pointed to a small black speck in the distant sky. "Is that an eagle?"

Dayna jerked back from Luke, breaking whatever spell he had cast over her. It had to be the exertion of the hike fogging her brain and making her see things that weren't really there.

She turned away from Luke and raised her binoculars. The black speck was indeed an eagle. "Yes, it is. Do either one of you know what kind of eagle?"

"It's a bald eagle," Todd said as he focused in on the bird. He glanced over his shoulder at his uncle. "He doesn't look too big to me, Uncle Luke."

Luke picked up his own binoculars and grinned. "That's because he's a long distance away. He probably has a nest down there near the lake. Bald eagles like to eat fish."

"He doesn't live up here?" Jesse asked.

"Afraid not. Bald eagles tend to build their nests close to rivers or lakes so they're close to the food supply."

Todd frowned. "So why is this called Bald Mountain if the bald eagle doesn't live here?"

Dayna heard the disappointment in her son's voice and tried to explain. "I'm not sure where the mountain got its name, Todd. But if the eagle had built its nest up here, he wouldn't have been very happy to see us. Eagles are very protective of their young. I'm sure Luke brought us up here so we could see the birds from this vantage point and admire the view." She glanced out at the valleys below and the mountains surrounding them and had to admit the view was well worth the climb.

"Your mother is right," Luke said. "I've never heard of an eagle attacking a human that got too close to its nest, but I'm sure it's happened. We wouldn't want to upset the eagle or make the babies have to wait for their meal. This is the perfect spot for watching them without interfering. If we hiked into the forest surrounding the lake down there, you wouldn't be able to see the birds at all, unless you took a boat out onto the lake. It's kind of like not being able to see the forest for the trees. You need to get to a higher elevation to see the whole forest."

"So how did the mountain get its name?" asked Jesse.

"An old miner named Baldy Johnson, back around 1881, discovered some gold in a small creek on the eastern side of the mountain. Nothing ever came of it, no mother lode, no more strikes, so the boom of prospectors moved on to greener pastures, leaving behind Baldy and his mountain."

Jesse looked disappointed. "They named it after a man named Baldy?"

Luke grinned. "Sure did. Over the years people referred to it as Bald Mountain instead of Baldy Mountain, but it's one and the same."

"That's cool," Todd said. "We own a town named after a poker hand." He glanced at his mother. "Hey, Mom, how did you name Jesse and me?"

"The way most mothers name their babies in

this century. I went to a bookstore and purchased a baby name book."

Jesse sighed. "Oh."

Dayna heard the disappointment in her younger son's voice. "You wanted to be named Baldy?"

Todd laughed and playfully punched Jesse in the arm. "He looks more like a poker hand to me, Mom."

"Jack's not a bad name," she said.

"I was thinking more along the lines of Joker." Todd's laughter again filled the air.

Jesse stuck out his tongue. "You look more like a Queenie than a Todd."

Dayna shook her head and grinned. Two years ago, when Steven was still alive and living with them, neither boy would argue or jest with the other one. Both boys had been quiet and withdrawn for fear of earning a reprimand from their father. It had taken two years for them to come out of their shells, but now she considered them healthy and normal boys. There were times when she wished for the quiet and reserved boys to come back, but those times were few and far between. She'd take their bickering and jokes any day.

"Hey, boys," Luke said as he pointed to the valley below. "It looks like mamma eagle is making another food run."

Everyone adjusted their binoculars and feasted on one of Mother Nature's wonderful sights.

❖━━━❖

Luke watched as Dayna policed the area for trash one last time before they started back down the mountain. The enticing view of her jean-clad bottom as she bent over was enough to raise his blood pressure. And it wasn't only his blood pressure he was in fear of rising. Being in Dayna's company for the past twenty-four hours had taught him one thing: The feelings he had for her were growing stronger by the minute. He wanted Dayna.

The attraction he felt for her was more than just physical. A physical, lustful relationship between a man and a woman he understood. He'd been experiencing those types of relationships for twenty years. A man had needs. A woman had needs. If the man and woman agreed, both needs could be met with respect, understanding, and satisfaction. It was all clean and simple. What he felt for Dayna was neither clean nor simple.

Every emotion he possessed was ricocheting around in some dense fog, that was only getting thicker by the hour. The complications were mounting by the minute. And in some dark corner of his mind, a voice was screaming that there was something decidedly sick about desiring your dead brother's wife. Then again, it had been even more warped to desire Dayna when Steven had been alive.

When she had told him she'd named him guardian of the boys, panic had seized his mind. Was she sick, dying? What did she know that no one else knew? After she'd assured him she was healthy and was only covering all the bases, common sense had calmed his terror. Dayna had only done the reasonable, mature thing; she'd made out a will. Everyone should have a will. He had a will.

He had just never given any thought to what parents did when there were children involved. Dayna must have been panic-stricken thinking about his mother getting her hands on the boys and turning them into miniature versions of Steven. He was honored and gratified that she thought highly enough of him to name him guardian, but he sure as hell didn't want anything to happen to her.

"We're ready to go now," she said.

Luke glanced off in the distance. They had plenty of daylight left. More than enough time to hike back down to where he had parked his Jeep and then drive the twenty minutes to Aces High. "We can stay another half hour if you like."

"No thanks. I'd like to be back at Aces High and be done with dinner before it gets too dark." She tugged on the baseball cap she had worn earlier and pulled her ponytail through the opening in the back.

He thought she looked sexy as hell, her face glowing with the sun-kissed flush of their hike, clunky hiking boots on her small feet, and jeans and a T-shirt molding her body like a pair of lover's hands. He didn't know of too many women who could pull off the outdoorsy look while actually living without any modern conveniences. Dayna was one of them. Then again, she had looked beautiful as a bride, radiant as an expectant mother, and dignified and composed as a widow. He had seen her at her best and at her worst, and never once considered her anything less than perfect. It was a scary thought.

"Can I lead the way back, Uncle Luke?" Todd asked.

He reached down and tousled the boy's dark hair. "You can lead for the first part, and then Jesse can lead for the second half." From what he could remember, Todd looked exactly like Steven had at his age. There had been a five-year age difference between Luke and Steven, and their personalities had been miles apart. When Steven was eight, Luke was thirteen and living at a private school on the outskirts of Denver. He'd only been allowed home on weekends and holidays. By that time Steven had not only taken over the house, but their mother's affection as well. Their father, who had still been alive, had been too busy between work and his newest mistress to notice or care about his sons.

Todd might look like Steven, but there the resemblance ended. Todd was neither spoiled, selfish, nor deceitful. Todd and Jesse loved each other as brothers should. When his mother had brought Steven home from the hospital, Luke had felt so proud and protective to be the older brother. Over the years the pride had been ground into ashes and the only protectiveness he now felt was geared toward Steven's sons.

Jesse ran up to him, all excited and filled with wonder at being in charge. "Can I really lead?"

"Sure can, Jess." He adjusted the crooked cap on Jesse's head and grinned.

"What if I get us lost?" Jesse's teeth sank into his lower lip, a trait Luke had noticed he'd inherited from his mother.

"How about if I keep an eye on things and if I notice we're heading in the wrong direction I'll tell you?"

"Great!"

The smile that broke across Jesse's face tugged at his heart. It reminded him of Dayna and the fact that his life back in Washington was so empty. Steven had had all of this and had thrown it away. There was a saying that one man's garbage was another man's treasure. He wondered how he was supposed to pick up the pieces Steven had so callously disregarded and convince them they were treasures?

He glanced over at Dayna, who had been watching him and the boys. A soft smile curved her mouth, and if he wasn't mistaken, a sheen of moisture was gleaming in her eyes. She met his gaze and silently mouthed one word—*thanks*.

He knew right then that he had indeed stumbled across a treasure. A treasure that would not only enlighten his world, but was more precious than gold.

FIVE

Dayna dunked Jesse's jeans into the creek one last time and frowned at the dirt stains still covering the knees. So much for the old-fashioned way of beating clothes against rocks to get them clean. The bar of environmentally safe soap might be good for the environment, but it was useless against the dirt Jesse could grind into a pair of jeans.

They had made it back from Bald Mountain with plenty of sunlight to spare, so she had called a bath night. Before Luke had arrived, she'd accompanied the boys to the creek and watched over them as they scrubbed themselves clean with cold water and shrieks of laughter. Tonight Luke had gone with the boys while she gathered up some firewood. The three males returned warm, clean, and with damp hair, and her sons were carrying another armful of dirty laundry.

As soon as they were settled back at camp, she'd

instructed Luke on what to make for dinner, then she had headed for the creek herself, loaded down with two pails of dirty laundry, soap, and a set of clean clothes for herself. She definitely missed an automatic washer, but she yearned for a nice hot shower more.

With a strong twist, she wrung out the jeans and tossed them into the bucket containing all the other clean laundry. The only other dirty clothes left to do were the ones she was wearing. Her hands were red from the chilly water and she wasn't looking forward to immersing her body in the creek. But vanity was a curse. If it were only she and her sons, she would consider a quick splash here and there and possibly renting a motel room for a night when they went into Meeker Park to buy some more food. But with Luke pitching his tent right next to theirs and initiating thigh-screaming hikes up the sides of mountains, a quick splash here and there just wouldn't do.

With a slight shudder she unsnapped her jeans, tossed them, and her T-shirt onto the bank, picked up a bottle of shampoo, and waded into the icy water.

Five minutes later her hair was washed and wrapped in a towel. Her jeans and shirt had been washed and added to the pile to be hung when she returned to camp. She was sitting on a rock, wearing nothing more than a bra and panties and looking nothing like an ad for Victoria's Secret. The phrase "freezing one's butt off" was taking on a new meaning. Could a person actually freeze to death while bathing in a mountain stream during the summer? How would her boys ever recover from discovering Mom, the frozen pop, standing in her unmentionables knee-deep in the creek?

She laughed at that ridiculous picture and reached for the bar of soap before she lost all feeling in her fingers and toes. Luke's voice stilled her hand.

"Dayna? Are you all right?"

She jerked her head around, but couldn't see him. As soon as her heart left her throat, she yelled, "Go away."

A low, deep chuckle emerged from the bushes at the top of the bank. "Don't worry, I haven't peeked."

She glanced down at what she considered her uninspiring breasts and soft stomach, complete with faded stretch marks, and sighed. She couldn't blame him. Who in the world would want to peek at her? "Good. Now go away."

His voice still held a note of laughter. "What's taking you so long? We were beginning to worry."

"I don't know. Maybe it's the two buckets of laundry I had to hand wash."

"Need any help?"

She glared at the bushes where his voice seemed to be coming from, but she couldn't see anything. She hoped he couldn't see anything either. "I'm all done with the wash. The only thing left to be cleaned is me."

Silence greeted that announcement, then he asked, "Still need any help?"

She didn't detect any laughter in his voice that time. What in the world was Luke doing? Was he flirting with her? Impossible! Maybe he thought his late brother's wife needed a little more comforting than was commonly acceptable. However, she didn't need or want a man in her life, especially one with the last name of Callahan.

"You better be careful what you offer, Luke. I'm a poor, defenseless widow trying to support two growing boys. I just may take you up on that offer and drag your sorry butt down the aisle." That should put a halt to any more of his suggestive comments, she thought. Mention marriage and any confirmed bachelor would run for the hills. Out here, there were plenty of hills to run to.

This time the silence lasted longer. "Still need any help?"

Dayna scowled at the bushes. So much for her knowledge and understanding of the male species. "Where are Jesse and Todd, Luke?"

The last thing she needed was for her sons to hear this ridiculous conversation. The main gist of it would probably go over their heads, but they might start connecting Luke and her. Todd and Jesse were so deprived of any male companionship, they tended to go to extremes. This past spring Todd had gotten it into his head that his Little League coach would make a perfect dad for him and Jesse. There had been a few embarrassing moments before she had figured out what was going on and had a heart-to-heart with Todd. He understood about the coach, but there had been a certain stubborn gleam in his eye regarding finding a dad. She didn't need that gleam to settle on Uncle Luke.

"They're setting out the kindling for tonight's fire," he answered.

"Then I suggest you go join them," she snapped. "I'll be up in a few more minutes."

"We'll have the fire going before you get back. You really should dry your hair before you catch your death." There was the distant sound of rustling leaves and then he was gone.

Dayna's mouth dropped open. How did he know she had just washed her hair? That sneak *had* peeked! Or he was one lucky guesser. As soon as the boys went to sleep that night, she was going to have a nice long chat with her ex-brother-in-law concerning privacy. Her privacy.

"Uncle Luke said he'll take us up to Cooper's Grave tomorrow," Todd said as he snuggled down into his sleeping bag for the night.

"I don't know about hiking to a place called Cooper's Grave to pan for gold, boys." She appreciated Luke's generous offer to take them to a spot that he considered more appropriate for finding gold nuggets. But the thought of another one of his *short* hikes and the name of the place was extremely dismaying. Add the fact that he hadn't cleared it with her before mentioning it to the boys, and that the chances of them following the creek up to Cooper's Grave were mighty slim.

"Oh, Mom," Jesse moaned. "You're not scared of ghosts, are you? You told me they weren't real."

She bent over and brushed a kiss across Jesse's cheek. How could she deny her sons anything so simple as a hike up another mountain? She had promised them an adventure, and an adventure they would have. The first day they had arrived in Aces High, they had explored every inch of the town and turned up nothing more thrilling than an old skeleton of what appeared to have been a fox.

"You're right, Jesse," she said. "There are no such things as ghosts. I guess a little hike up to Cooper's Grave won't hurt us, but remember, you both promised to help carry the panning sieves."

"Great!" Todd shouted as he shot a look of triumph at his little brother. "See, I told you she'd let us."

Jesse grinned back. "Maybe tomorrow we'll find the mother lode. The first thing I'll buy when we get rich is Disneyland."

Todd laughed. "Not me. I'm buying the Denver Broncos. That way I'll get to see all their games and maybe John Elway will give me his autograph."

Dayna chuckled and picked up the lantern and her hairbrush. "Both of you get some sleep. Tomorrow looks like it will be another long day."

Her thighs were still aching from that day's hike up Bald Mountain. She didn't know how she was going to manage another uphill climb, even if Luke insisted that this hike would be like a walk in the park. Somehow she had the sinking feeling that Luke's park and her park weren't anything alike. If they did strike the mother lode tomorrow the first thing she would buy would be a hot tub.

" 'Night, Mom," Todd mumbled as he rolled onto his side and closed his eyes.

Jesse yawned and snuggled into his pillow. " 'Night, Mom."

"Good night, boys." She unzipped the tent flap and carried the lit lantern back outside. The cool evening air had her yanking up the zipper of her jacket and yearning for that hot tub.

She glanced around their campsite, making sure everything was secure for the night. Dinner had been cleaned up over an hour ago. The food was all packed away into the Blazer, the laundry was strung out between the porch posts of the saloon, and the panning equipment was piled neatly into a cardboard box sitting on the saloon's deteriorating porch.

Luke was stretched out in his chair with his boots nearly in the low burning flames of their fire. He appeared to be asleep, his dark lashes feathering his high cheekbones. The glow from the fire softened his hard features. Looking at him now she would never have figured him to be Steven's brother. The rich brown hair and dark eyes were the same, but that was where the similarities ended.

Steven had been a *boyishly* handsome man with a quick smile and flirtatious charm. Over the years the smile, the charm, and even his good looks as well as his body had softened. When Steven died he was thirty-one years old, still trying to appear twenty-two, and failing miserably.

No one would dare classify Luke as *boyishly* handsome. His face was arresting in its masculinity. Dark shadow constantly blanketed his jaw, no matter how recently he'd shaved. His piercing eyes seemed to take in everything around him. She had a feeling nothing and no one got by Luke. Steven, on the other hand, had been a sucker. He would fall for any scam that promised him quick, easy money. Why in the hell had she fallen for a man like Steven? Why couldn't she have fallen in love with someone like Luke? Someone who was strong, dependable, and could smell a con a mile away.

Dayna shook her head and glared at Luke. Damn him for showing her the errors of her youth. At twenty-two she had been swept off her feet by Steven's easygoing charm, kisses that promised heaven, and the idea that they both wanted the same things out of life; a nice home, children, and a lasting love. She'd found out much later that Steven had wanted quite different things—that is, a malleable wife who would provide him with a comfortable home and sex whenever he wanted it. His mistake, he'd told her mockingly the night he left, was she'd been the wrong woman all along.

Having Luke show up at Aces High was just one more reminder of how she had failed. She had failed Steven by not being woman enough. Failed her marriage by expecting too much from it. But most importantly, she had failed her sons. They were too young to be without a father, and she had thrown Steven out of the house months before his death. She had deprived her sons of the remaining months of Steven's life.

It didn't matter that Steven had been a terrible father. He was the only one the boys would have. She should have hung in there and tried harder. Maybe if she had, Steven wouldn't have been out carousing at a bar at two in the morning and in no condition to drive his car that rainy night.

She nudged Luke's foot a little harder than she should have. "You're going to melt the soles of your boots if you aren't careful." It would be one way to get out of hiking tomorrow, but she didn't relish the idea of driving him all the way into Boulder to see a doctor about his burned feet.

She tossed two more logs onto the fire, turned her folding chair around so her back was facing the flames, and sat down. Yanking the elastic band from her hair, she allowed the hair to tumble down past her shoulders. Her damp hair. She should have known there wasn't going to be enough daylight left to dry it. It irked her that she had to use the fire Luke and the boys had built to finish drying the damp strands. With a weary sigh she set the brush in motion, tried to shrug off the feeling of being a failure, and contemplated the stars.

"You don't dye your hair, do you?" Luke asked.

The rhythmic strokes she had been applying to

her hair faltered, but she didn't turn around. "What kind of question is that to ask a woman?" She had seen his feet pull back when she'd added the logs to the fire, so she'd known he wasn't asleep. Still his voice startled her more than the question. Ever since she'd returned to camp after taking her bath, she hadn't been able to meet his gaze. The thought of him spying on her while she had been bathing was both humiliating and infuriating.

"I swear, Dayna, I didn't look." He sighed. "I'm a little old to go around hiding in the bushes and checking out naked women as they splash around in a stream."

"I wasn't naked." She had had her bra and panties on while he had been there. But soaked silk and lace didn't leave a lot to the imagination.

"So why are you in such a snit if you weren't naked?"

"Keep your voice down!" she whispered. She didn't need Todd or Jesse getting the impression Luke had seen her naked. She went back to brushing her hair. The faster it dried, the faster she could call it a night.

A few minutes later Luke mumbled, "Now I'm really confused."

"About what?" As far as she was concerned, Luke could stay confused for the rest of his life, but she was curious as to what could possibly have confused him.

"How did you take a bath if you weren't naked?"

Okay, so maybe the creep hadn't been spying on

her. But that left an even more disturbing reason for him to come down to the creek. He had been worried about her. She knew her sons well enough to realize that if Luke was with them, they wouldn't be concerned about her. No, it was Luke who had been worried. She didn't want Luke, or any other man, worrying about her. She could take care of herself.

"Listen, Luke, if you're going to be staying here with us we need to discuss some rules."

"What kind of rules?"

She could feel his gaze on her as she continued to brush her hair. "Privacy rules."

"I only went down to the creek to make sure you were all right, not to get a cheap thrill."

"I've been taking care of myself for a long time, Luke. I don't need you following me around." She shoved her fingers into her hair and silently groaned at the dampness she still felt.

"He really did a job on you, didn't he?"

"I'd rather not talk about Steven. He's dead, let him rest in peace."

"Why should he be able to rest in peace while you're living with the consequences?"

The brush slipped from her fingers and landed in the dirt as she jerked her head around to glare at him. "What consequences?" The only thing she was living with were her sons. Todd and Jesse weren't hers or anyone else's consequences. They were her life.

Luke stood up and walked over to her. Bending, he picked up the black bristled brush and dusted it off with the sleeve of his sweatshirt. He had obviously touched another nerve with Dayna. Hell, that's all he had been doing since he'd arrived at Aces High, hitting one nerve after another. Dayna had more touchy subjects than a presidential candidate.

He tested the weight of the brush in his hand while contemplating Dayna's shimmering hair. The silky golden tresses gleamed in the firelight. The unexpected urge to run the brush through her hair slammed into his gut. He'd had lovers before, but never once had he fantasized about brushing their hair. He wondered what Dayna would do if he asked to brush her hair. Probably pack up the boys and head out of there. It was bad enough she thought he'd sneak around in bushes, spying on her while she bathed.

He reached out and fingered a golden strand. "You have beautiful hair."

She jerked her head around farther, effectively removing her hair from his fingers. "Don't change the subject, Luke. What consequences?"

He dropped his hand. "One being you can't accept a compliment. When a man tells you you have gorgeous hair, you're supposed to say thank you."

She reached up and, with angry jerks, wrapped the elastic band around her hair. "It's been my experience that compliments usually come with a price tag."

He wondered what kind of price tags his brother had placed on them. Dayna was acting as skittish as a deer sensing a nearby wolf. "When I give a compliment, it's freely given. No price tags. No favors to return." He gave her what he hoped was his best smile. "But a thank-you would have been nice."

She stood and stepped back from him. "Thank you." She took the brush he held out to her. "I think I'll be calling it a night. It's my impression that we'll be hiking up to Cooper's Grave tomorrow."

Her moving away from him hurt. Dayna was always stepping away from him. What did she think? That he had some type of contagious disease? "Is there a reason you dislike me besides my having the misfortune of being Steven's brother?"

"Who said I didn't like you?"

He took a step forward and frowned as she immediately took another step back. "Are you afraid of me?" He tried to read the expression on her face but couldn't. She had moved out of the circle of light from the fire. For one terrifying moment he pictured Steven hitting Dayna. As far as he knew, his brother hadn't been a physically abusive person. Steven's specialty had been more emotional. He had loved playing mind games and jerking people's chains. But Luke hadn't even known Dayna and Steven had been separated. What else didn't he know?

She slowly shook her head. "No, Luke. I'm not afraid of you."

He forced himself to take a step closer. This time she didn't back away or flinch. Reaching up, he tenderly traced the curve of her cheek. "Did he hit you?"

"No."

He felt the shiver that shook her body as he cupped her cheek and stepped closer still. He was undecided if it was his nearness that caused her to tremble, or distant memories, or the chill of the night air. "You don't have to lie, Dayna. There's nothing I can do to him now." *Except curse his soul to hell.* His heart seemed to have risen to his throat where it lodged and prevented him from swallowing. It was vitally important to his peace of mind to know if Steven had physically abused Dayna.

She shook her head again and whispered, "Steven never raised his hand in anger to me or the boys."

"There are other ways to hurt people, though. Steven was a master at finding someone's weak spot and playing it for all it was worth."

She tried to turn her head away, but he wouldn't let her. "Was he?" she asked, her voice soft and trembling.

"Did he find your weak spot, Dayna?"

She looked off to the side without saying a word.

Luke followed her gaze to the distant mountain peaks. It was so dark out that it was nearly impossible to tell where the mountains ended and the night sky began. His gaze returned to her face, but he couldn't see anything besides the general outline of her features. He could feel her trembling increase. His brother had pounced on Dayna's weakest spot as a starving leopard would spring onto a slab of raw meat. His arms ached from not being able to hold her and tell her everything was going to be all right, that Steven would never hurt her again. What Dayna needed was to talk about it. Get it all out in the open. That way the wounds Steven had inflicted wouldn't fester and the healing could begin. Perhaps then she might be able to start another relationship.

"Want to tell me about it?" he asked. The chances of Dayna telling him anything were small to nonexistent, but he had to try.

She jerked her head back around and turned the tables on him. "Did he find your vulnerable spot and use it against you, Luke?"

He couldn't blame her asking. It seemed only fair. "Yes, he did."

The anger was gone from her voice as she asked, "You have a weak spot?"

"You don't have to sound so surprised. Everyone has something that could bring them to their knees." He dropped his hand from her face as one of the logs she had tossed onto the fire flared up. He could see the uncertainty growing in her eyes. Did she honestly think he was so inhuman as to not have a soft spot?

"What's yours?" she asked.

He closed his eyes and prayed for guidance. None came. Should he lie or tell the truth? Was she ready to hear the truth? Somehow he had the feeling Dayna would never be ready to hear the truth, yet it was beyond him to lie to her. He would rather cut out his own heart than to hurt her by lying. He opened his eyes and gave her the power to bring him to his knees. "You are my weakness."

"Me?"

He almost chuckled at the astonishment in her voice. "Yes, you."

"I don't understand."

"Join the club." He didn't understand it either. He knew he and Dayna had a lot in common. They both appreciated, even loved, history. They both were intelligent, responsible, and caring individuals. They even shared a frustrating relationship with Eileen Callahan. But he knew his fascination with Dayna went far beyond common interests. It had since he'd first met her.

Somewhere along the way his guard had slipped where she was concerned, and Steven had picked up on Luke's desire for his wife. His brother had gleefully used that knowledge to his advantage for years, usually to get Luke to loan him money for another one of his ill-advised schemes.

"Steven knew I cared about you," Luke said. "He had been emotionally blackmailing me with that knowledge for years."

"I still don't understand." She nervously chewed on her lower lip. "How could he use your affection for your sister-in-law against you?"

"My affections for you have nothing to do with you being my sister-in-law." How could she be so blind? Didn't she realize what she did to him?

"They don't?"

"Oh, hell!" He was tired of trying to explain it all to her. "Maybe this will show you what I'm talking about." He hauled her into his arms and claimed her mouth with the fierce need that had been building for years.

SIX

The shock of Luke's kiss held Dayna immobile for five full seconds before her brain kicked in. Luke was kissing her! Her mind told her to push him away, but her body was sending a very different message. Heat, unlike anything she had ever experienced, melted her resistance until she could do nothing but wrap her arms around Luke's neck to keep from dissolving into a puddle at his feet.

The sweep of his tongue against her lips sent every hormone she possessed scrambling out of its protective shell. Sweet fire scorched her as she slowly opened her mouth and allowed Luke entrance. The feel of his hands caressing her back made her yearn for something more. Even through the layers of her jacket and sweatshirt she could feel his heat. Feel his need.

She met every bold stroke of his tongue with one of her own. A moan trembled in the back of her throat, matched by a deep groan from Luke as he pulled her closer and deepened the kiss. Dayna felt whatever resistance she had left ebb away on the tide of desire Luke's kisses had generated. Wherever he wanted to lead, she was more than willing to follow. She had to see where this would all end.

A murmur of dismay tumbled from her lips as he broke the kiss and put a few inches between them. Her hands shook as she tried to pull him back.

He reached up and gently disengaged her hold from around his neck. "Now do you understand?" he asked, his voice rough, uneven.

She swept her tongue across her lips; his taste clung to her. The night was obscuring her vision. She couldn't read Luke's face, but she could hear his breathing. He sounded like he had just scaled Pikes Peak. And though she wasn't an expert on the male anatomy, when she had been plastered against his body a moment ago she had felt his response to her. His rigid, jean-bulging response. Luke had been just as affected by the kiss as she had. So why had he stopped?

Strands of hair escaped her hastily constructed ponytail as she shook her head in confusion. She didn't understand anything that was happening. Luke had kissed her and she felt like she had just awakened from a long sleep. "No," she whispered, though she wasn't sure what she was denying.

He thrust his hand through his hair while muttering a curse that made her flinch. "Dammit,

Dayna, you can't be that naive and innocent not to know what just happened."

She hadn't been innocent or naive in a very long time. "I know what happened."

"What?"

"You kissed me."

"And?"

She worried her lower lip and wondered how she'd gotten herself into this mess. She had just kissed her brother-in-law. Well, technically, Luke wasn't her brother-in-law any longer, but he was her sons' uncle. Worse than that, he was a Callahan, and a Callahan was the same as trouble. Hadn't she learned anything during her marriage to Steven? Lord, what had she done?

"And—and what?" she asked.

"What else happened besides me kissing you?"

She straightened her shoulders and raised her chin. "I kissed you back." *There, she'd admitted it!* Now maybe he would leave her alone so she could go contemplate what kind of insanity had just overruled her head and stirred her hormones.

His voice softened. "Yes, you did, Dayna. We shared a kiss." He glanced over at the tent where the boys lay sleeping. "You felt it, too, didn't you?"

"Felt what?" Why couldn't he just write it off as a simple kiss and forget that it ever happened? Why was he pushing so hard?

"The heat! The desire!" His voice rose like thunder, deep with intensity, but low in volume. "You can't deny what you felt, Dayna. I held your body and felt your response. You wanted me as much as I wanted you."

"I don't—"

"Don't lie to me, Dayna." He shook his head and took a step back. "Lie to yourself, if you must. But don't lie to me. I wanted you from the first moment I saw you, nine years ago, and the feeling hasn't died. While you were Steven's wife I could deny the attraction by placing as much distance between us as possible. But not now. Steven isn't here any longer, Dayna. There's only you and me." He glanced at her tent again as if wanting to say something about the boys, but didn't. "When you've figured out what you want and aren't afraid to admit it, let me know." With that, he turned and walked away.

She watched as darkness swallowed him. He was wrong. She hadn't been about to lie to him. She was going to tell him once again that she didn't understand what had happened when they had kissed, but now it was too late. She was beginning to understand, and it was scaring the hell out of her. Luke Callahan wanted her, and her treacherous body had wanted him in return.

If it wasn't so mind-boggling, she would have laughed herself sick. Another Callahan male was about to make her life a living nightmare, only this time she wasn't some innocent twenty-two-year-old who thought passion-filled kisses held the future. She knew better. The passion she and Steven had shared had died a slow, agonizing death.

Dayna shivered at the humiliating memories of her trying to rekindle that passion. Returning to the fire, she threw another log onto the flames and sat down. What was she going to do? Luke had obviously wanted her tonight. There were just some reactions a man was incapable of faking. But to consider seriously that he had been attracted to her for the past nine years was ridiculous. The man who had pledged his undying love to her hadn't been attracted to her for even half that length of time.

The Luke she had come to know over the years wouldn't lie. He was too proud and honorable. On the other hand, she also knew him to be a successful, confident, not to mention heart-stoppingly handsome man. Why would someone like Luke want her?

Dayna picked up the scorched twig Todd had been using to toast marshmallows and tossed it into the fire. The gooey clump of sugar on the end flared briefly and died. She glanced at the electric-blue-and-green tent where her sons slept. They worshiped the ground their uncle walked on, and she would do everything in her power to keep it that way. Todd and Jesse needed a male figure to look up to and Luke was the obvious choice. She had to convince Luke that his fascination with her, while flattering, was unwarranted and that their kiss had been a mistake. One she was not willing to repeat.

She glanced off in the direction in which he had disappeared, and frowned. Nothing was out there but uneven terrain and trees. Without a flashlight,

Luke could very easily sprain an ankle or worse. What in the heck had he been thinking when he stormed off like that?

With a deep sigh she rose, picked up the lantern, and headed after him. Four minutes later she found him sitting on a boulder surveying the star-strewn heavens.

Luke heard Dayna coming before he saw light from her lantern. He was hoping she was ready to admit that she wanted him, but he figured that would be classed well beyond wishful thinking. Knowing Dayna, she was probably worried he'd trip over a root and break his leg. Whoever had passed out the maternal instincts had given Dayna more than her fair share. And the last thing he wanted from her was mothering.

The cry of a nearby owl caused her to jump just as she reached him. He smiled. "Relax. It's only the same owl you've been hearing every night."

"I know," she said as she placed the lantern on a flat rock near his feet. "He just sounded closer than I expected."

He nodded toward a clump of trees to his right. "He's in there, but I haven't been able to spot him yet."

"He's probably a she, and she's probably sitting on a nest."

Her gaze left the trees, and she seemed to be studying the rock he was sitting on. Great! he thought. She wouldn't even look at him now. How could whatever relationship he had with her have deteriorated further? The next thing he'd know she'd be pleading with him to just be friends. That's when he would hit rock bottom.

"Did you come looking for me to discuss the wildlife?"

"Ah . . . no." She jammed her hands into the pockets of her jacket but didn't raise her gaze above his knees. "I think we need to talk."

"About?" His stomach clenched as he felt the "let's be friends" speech coming.

"What happened earlier." Her gaze darted back in the direction she had come.

"The hike to Bald Mountain?"

"Not that."

"The fact that I promised Todd and Jesse a trip to Cooper's Grave tomorrow without clearing it with you first?" He knew he should have discussed it with her before mentioning it to the boys, but she had been down at the creek at the time. His mind had been so busy wandering to crystal clear water and one lucky bar of soap, he hadn't been thinking clearly where Todd and Jesse were concerned.

"We'll talk about that later," she said, "but that's not why I came out here now."

"Then why did you come?" He knew why, but he wasn't going to help her out. It would be like shooting himself in the foot.

"Couldn't we just forget what happened back at the campfire?" She gave a slight shrug. "You know, pretend it didn't happen and go on being friends."

"No." There it was, the sound of him hitting

rock bottom. He watched as her shocked gaze jerked up to meet his, and he almost grinned as her mouth dropped open. Here he was, thirty-seven years old, and the woman he desired wanted to be friends. This was as low as it got, and he'd be damned before he agreed to such an asinine suggestion. "That kiss was very, very real, Dayna, and there is no way I will forget it. As it stands, I want you, you wanted me. Now the question is, what are you going to do about it?"

"Me?"

"You already know what I want to do about it." Actually, he wanted to do a lot more with Dayna besides make love to her. But if she was this panicky over a kiss, he couldn't imagine what her reaction would be if he dared breathe the word "future."

"Well, you can't always get what you want."

He raised a brow at the well-known lyric from a Rolling Stones' song. "Tell me about it. I've been living with that truth for nine years."

Dayna's hands left her pockets to wave uselessly in the air. "Stop saying that."

"Why?"

"Because"—her voice rose to a high-pitched wail—"it can't be true."

"Why can't it be true?" She sounded frustrated and confused, but not horrified. He wondered if that was a good sign.

"Why didn't you say anything before now?" she asked.

"When exactly was I supposed to say something?

During the rehearsal dinner for your wedding to my brother? How about when the minister asked if there was anyone with just cause as to why the wedding shouldn't take place?" He shook his head. "Was I supposed to say excuse me, but Steven can't marry you because I want to ask you out?"

"You wanted to go out with me during my wedding?"

"Dayna, I'm trying to be a gentleman here. Sitting across from you in some fancy restaurant discussing current events was the furthest thing from my mind."

He watched as her teeth worried her lower lip for a full minute. "So all this"—her arm waved between him and their campsite—"is about lust?"

"No. Yes." He ran his hands down his face and prayed for strength. "Oh, hell. Yes, Dayna, this is partially about lust, but only a very small part."

"What's the large part about?"

"I don't know. That's what I've been trying to figure out." He studied her face in the faint glow of the lantern. She was the most beautiful woman he'd ever seen. Her chin was a little too pointy, her mouth was on the generous side and slightly swollen now from his kisses and her habit of chewing on her lower lip when upset. Her hair was pulled away from her face in a haphazard ponytail that made her look nineteen. There even appeared to be a smudge of dirt on her cheek. But she was still the most beautiful woman he had ever seen. Her eyes were the color of the morning skies over the mountains, and they were the clearest and most honest eyes he had ever encountered. Her every emotion was mirrored in those eyes. Now they were showing her confusion.

"Yes, I want you in my bed, Dayna. I can't deny that. But I also want you in my life. In the past nine years I've compared every woman I met to you and each one came up lacking. I have to know if that's because you're the woman I need, or because I'm incapable of sustaining a relationship with a woman." He reached out a hand toward her. "I need to make you happy. I need to make up for the hell Steven put you through. I need a lot of things I'm just beginning to realize."

She glanced at his extended hand and took a step back as if it were a snake. "That's what all this is about, isn't it? Steven's no longer around, so you're going to pick up all the pieces and make things right. Give poor Dayna a man and Todd and Jesse the father figure they never had." She took another step back. "I know all about when you and Steven were boys and how you were always there to clean up his messes and fix his problems."

She shook her head as tears pooled in her eyes. "I'm not stupid, Luke. I also know about the mysterious backer who stepped in three years ago and pulled Steven's butt out of a financial screwup. I know you were that backer."

"You were about to lose the house, Dayna! I couldn't allow you and the boys to be tossed out into the street. Why didn't you call me?"

"It wasn't your problem. How did you hear about it?"

"Sam Altman, an old family friend, gave me a call." He ran a hand through his hair in frustration. How had the conversation gone from a future with Dayna to the past and Steven? "Sam handled the paperwork, I supplied the cash to bail Steven out. How did you know it was me?"

"You were the only one who cared enough. I put two and two together and came up with you."

"I didn't give a damn about Steven and what the creditors would have done to him. I have very deep feelings for you and the boys, Dayna. Don't you understand? I didn't want you to suffer because of my brother's stupidity."

"So now you feel responsible for me?" She swiped at the tears overflowing her eyes with the sleeve of her jacket. "I'm just another mess your brother left behind? Well, you can take your self-righteous attitude and your unwanted advances and go jam them up your . . ." She choked on the last word and wailed, "you know where." She turned to flee.

Luke propelled himself off the boulder and captured her arm. "If all I felt for you and the boys was responsibility, I'd write you a fat check to clear my mind."

She jerked her arm, trying to break his hold. "Oh, that's right. Your feelings go much deeper." She sent a scalding glance down his body to his crotch. "So deep they're all resting in your pants."

He released her arm as if she'd burned him. Dayna had the right to be a little upset or wary of him. After all, he had sprung this on her all of a sudden. He'd had nine years to confront the attraction he felt for her. She'd had exactly half an hour. But still, her insult cut deeply. "It seems I was wrong. My feelings weren't that deep after all." He watched as the anger fled her face. "They seemed to have stopped somewhere around here." He raised his fist and pressed it against his chest.

The instant her teeth sank into her lower lip, he turned and headed back to their camp. The only teeth he wanted sinking into that soft pink lip were his own. It now appeared that would never happen. Dayna would never be able to separate him from his brother.

He should have known it would be hopeless. Any relationship between a woman and a Callahan man was doomed from the beginning. Grandfather Max had had enough wives and mistresses to make a sultan jealous. Each one had left cursing the Callahan name, but a little bit richer than the one before her. His own parents' marriage had been a constant battle. Joseph Callahan slept in more beds than George Washington, and his mother had known it. Their public quarrels were notorious. He had hoped Steven's marriage would be better for Dayna's sake. Obviously, it hadn't been.

He kicked the campfire apart, leaving burning embers scattered within the rock circle the boys had built. He folded up the chairs and leaned them against the bumper of his Jeep. The camp was secure for the night. He glanced in the direction where he had left Dayna. The lantern was moving closer. She was returning to camp, but he was in no mood for the next round of "Pummel His Heart To Hell and Back," so he entered his tent and called it a night.

The next afternoon Dayna wearily returned to the camp and lowered the backpack from her sore shoulders. The boys and Luke had headed for the creek to wash up and she had the camp to herself. The hike to Cooper's Grave hadn't been nearly as bad as she had feared. It was the fact that she hadn't gotten one minute of sleep the night before that had done her in. How could she sleep after what had transpired between her and Luke?

Luke hadn't made the day any easier for her. He had been his same cheery self with the boys while politely ignoring her. The three males had joked and laughed the entire day. Luke had answered a billion questions without once losing his patience. He'd pointed out animal tracks, poisonous plants, and seemed to be a walking encyclopedia on local Indian lore. They had panned for hours up at Cooper's Grave, which contrary to its name, didn't contain any noticeable grave. Thank the Lord. Seemed a miner named Cooper had dug himself a nearby mine shaft and had been searching for a dream. A local trapper had discovered the caved-in mine, no signs of Cooper, and had christened the place Cooper's Grave.

The boys had wanted to explore the entrance of the mine, but Luke hadn't let them anywhere near it, no matter how much they pleaded and begged. The love he felt for his nephews was evident in everything he did. He obviously liked kids and had the temperament to be a great father. So why hadn't he married and had a couple of children of his own? Dayna had wondered on and off during the day. It was a disturbing thought, considering what he'd admitted to her the night before. Luke had been comparing other women to her. How could he have done that, when he didn't know the real Dayna? Most of the time she didn't know the real Dayna.

The woman that she was today had only started to emerge within the last two years. Hell, half the time she still seemed to be stumbling through life, second-guessing every decision she made. Was she raising the boys all right? Did they need something she wasn't providing in the way of emotional support? Had she damaged their minds by throwing their father out of the house? Was their lukewarm grieving over their father's death natural, or a sign of deep emotional problems?

So many decisions to make, and all of them were hers. Had the plumber overcharged when he'd fixed her leaking kitchen sink, or did all plumbers charge more than doctors? Was she depriving her sons of a natural part of childhood by not allowing them to get a dog? On the one hand she wanted the boys to know the love and responsibility of owning a pet, but on the other hand it didn't seem fair to the poor dog to be left alone most of the day. Just once she would love to sit down with another adult and discuss these worries and the hundred more that popped up on a daily basis.

Luke would probably make a very good listener and adviser if she asked for his opinion. But it also seemed unfair to burden him with her problems just because he had the misfortune of being Steven's brother. Hadn't Luke endured enough because of Steven?

After the rosiness of romance had faded from her marriage, she had seen more clearly. Luke wasn't the arrogant older brother who had deserted his mother and taken off for the East Coast to make his own fortune, as Steven had told her. She witnessed first-hand the difference in Eileen's behavior toward her two sons. Eileen seemed to ignore Luke while she fawned over Steven. The unfairness of it had struck her on more than one occasion, and she couldn't understand why Luke would want to have anything to do with Steven's family.

It didn't make any sense. Nothing was making sense any longer. The more she thought about it, the more confused she became. Last night, lying in the dark and listening to the hoot of the owl and the gentle noises her sons made as they slept, she had forced all thoughts from her mind and concentrated on one thing. The kiss she had shared with Luke.

She had never experienced anything so mind-shattering in her life. She didn't know what upset her the most: The fact that she had actively participated in the kiss, that it was Luke she had been kissing, or that she hadn't wanted the kiss to end. All three were thought-provoking in themselves, but put them together and they spelled trouble. It didn't matter that trouble was the last thing she was looking for; it had found her. In the middle of the Rockies, in a deserted ghost town, trouble had found her, and he didn't appear to be packing his bags to leave.

What was she going to do if Luke hadn't been lying? What if he really had been attracted to her for the past nine years and was not just feeling responsible? That wasn't something she could ignore. Luke was family and they would be running into each other for years to come. They needed to talk about this attraction, bring it out into the open, so they could both honestly deal with it.

Her advice to Luke would be to get a grip on whatever insanity was polluting his mind and go out and find himself a wife who would give him half a dozen kids of his own to go camping with. As soon as he created his own family, he would stop wanting to be a part of hers.

The advice sounded logical and reasonable to her except for one minor detail. She wanted Luke to kiss her again so she could see if perhaps she wasn't blowing all of this out of proportion. Maybe his kiss had affected her so strongly because it had been one heck of a long time since a man had kissed her, or maybe it was just the pure shock of the whole thing.

Not many women had their brother-in-law kiss them. Either way, she wanted to experience his kiss again and that was a revelation in itself. For the first time in years, she actually wanted a man's kiss.

She heard Jesse's and Todd's laughter as they headed back toward camp. She didn't want to spend the night sitting around the campfire being ignored by Luke and her sons. This vacation had been her idea. This was her time to spend with her boys, strengthening the bonds between them. Luke shouldn't have come. He was not only confusing her hormones into wanting things they couldn't have, he was ruining her vacation.

SEVEN

"Are you sure you boys don't want another cup of hot chocolate?" Dayna asked. The night was coming to a close and she wasn't looking forward to when the boys went to bed, leaving her alone with Luke. He had been giving her peculiar looks all evening. Normally she wouldn't dream of overfilling the boys with something as sugary as hot chocolate before they went to bed, but she was desperate.

"No thanks, Mom," Todd said.

Jesse mumbled his negative response around a yawn.

Dayna frowned. What was she doing to her sons? It was already half an hour past their bedtime and they had hiked to Cooper's Grave and back that day. What kind of mother was she to hide behind two small boys? She was acting like a coward. It was about time she took charge of the situation. "Come on, boys, it's past your bedtime."

Jesse got up and made his way to the tent.

Todd looked at Luke. "Hey, Uncle Luke, what are we doing tomorrow?"

Over the top of Todd's head Dayna glared at Luke. Not "Mom, what are we doing tomorrow?" but "Hey, Uncle Luke!" It was as if she wasn't even there.

Luke glanced from Dayna back to Todd. "I don't know, Todd. Maybe your mother has already made some plans."

Todd looked over his shoulder at her. "Did you?"

Dayna bit the inside of her lip. He didn't have to sound so forlorn at the possibility that she had plans for them all. They had been managing just fine before Luke showed up. "I was thinking that maybe tomorrow we would take it easy and explore the town some more."

"We already did that," Todd complained.

She looked over at Luke. He was frowning at Todd, apparently unhappy that Todd considered any suggestion of hers dull compared to his. At least he appeared not to want to outdo her in front of her sons. And he had been awfully nice to the boys the past few days.

She glanced down at Todd. "Maybe, if Uncle Luke agrees, we can go exploring in the saloon and the house."

She gave Luke a tentative smile. "I would only allow them on the first floor before. If you're willing to check out the second floors for safety, I'd be willing to let them go exploring some more."

"Can we really?" Jesse shouted, who had been standing by the tent listening to the exchange.

"If Uncle Luke says it's safe, I don't see why not."

"I'll check it out," Luke said, "but if I say it isn't safe, there'll be no one going up there." He gave both boys a long look before glancing at her. "I mean no one."

She nodded, understanding his message. Not only were the boys not allowed up onto the second floor if he felt it was unsafe, neither was she. She had no problem with that. Peeking in empty, dust-coated bedrooms held absolutely no appeal to her if it meant she might go crashing through the floorboards. "It's settled then," she said. "Tomorrow after breakfast we explore the Rock Gut Saloon and in the afternoon we investigate the house."

Both boys jumped up and gave a shout of joy that probably frightened every animal within half a mile of their camp. "'Night, Mom," Todd said. "Thanks, Uncle Luke, for being here. If it weren't for you, we'd never get to explore the really neat stuff."

"Now, Todd, your mother is right in not letting you boys go where it might be unsafe. And it hasn't been determined if you'll be allowed to explore the 'really neat stuff' yet. I haven't seen the upstairs of the saloon in over fifteen years. It might not be safe any longer."

"But we are going to try, right?"

"Yes, I'll check it for structural damage, but your mother gets to make the final call."

"Oh, okay." Todd wished them both a final good night and disappeared into the tent. Jesse was right on his heels. As soon as the tent was zipped shut, their excitement was expressed with gales of laughter, an impromptu wrestling match, and what appeared to be a laser light show cast by their flashlights.

Dayna watched as the boys finally settled down. She had once again taken second place in her sons' eyes. She should be happy that both Todd and Jesse were bonding with an adult male. So why did she feel let down?

The food from their campfire snacks was still sitting out on the tailgate of her Blazer. She walked over to it and started to stack the remaining marshmallows, fruit cups, and the instant hot cocoa mix back into a cardboard box. The pot of coffee was on a rock near the fire keeping warm. She glanced over her shoulder at Luke, and found him watching her. "Want another cup of coffee before I pack it away?" It was the first time she had actually talked to him that day without having the boys as a buffer.

"I'll pour us both a cup. Why don't you go and tuck in the Land Barons for the night."

Luke had christened the boys with that ridiculous nickname because of their ownership of Aces High, and both boys loved it. She nodded. "I'll be right back."

She entered the tent and felt immediately better.

Both of the boys had been waiting for her and their good-night kiss. "Do either of you have to make a call to nature?" Every night she asked the same question and every night she had to wake up at least once and accompany one of the boys to the bushes.

"Nope," Todd said.

Jesse yawned. "Not me."

"Hey, Mom," Todd said. "Can Uncle Luke come with us on all our vacations?"

Dayna cringed. She knew Todd's voice had carried to the campfire. The only time her children whispered was around Christmastime and then it was only because they still believed in Santa. Luke was probably listening to every word of this conversation. "Luke has his own life to live, Todd. I'm sure he would rather spend his hard-earned vacations doing something more exciting than camping with his nephews and their mother."

"But Uncle Luke likes us, Mom," Jesse said.

"I know he does, honey." She brushed a golden lock of hair off Jesse's brow. "It doesn't mean that Uncle Luke doesn't like you if he goes somewhere else for his vacations. It just means he has different tastes than us. Not everyone likes to camp."

"But Uncle Luke says he loves to camp and he doesn't get to do it very often." Todd gave his mother a serious look.

"That's because he works very hard back in Washington." How had she ended up on the defensive end of this conversation? Todd was acting as if it was all her fault that Luke didn't get to go camping more.

"No, it's not," Todd said.

"It's not?"

"No. Uncle Luke told me he doesn't get to go camping very much because he doesn't have anyone to go camping with. He said it isn't as much fun all by yourself."

"He may be right about that, Todd." She pulled Jesse's sleeping bag all the way up to his chin. "Maybe one day Uncle Luke will have a family of his own to take camping."

"Why can't we be his family?" Todd's eyes seemed to glow with some inner excitement. "He needs a family to take on vacation and we need a dad."

"You need a dad?" Her heart rate had quadrupled at Todd's suggestion that they become Luke's family, then it had plummeted to her knees with his confession that he needed a dad. She was a lousy single parent after all. Why else would he need a dad?

"Justin says I'm never going to make any of the teams if I don't have a dad."

"Why not," she asked, "and what teams are you talking about?"

"Soccer is starting pretty soon and then there's baseball next spring."

"You don't need a dad to make those teams, Todd." She smiled. "You can play any sport you want, honey."

"Justin says I won't be able to play because I need to practice."

"Justin's only partly right, Todd. Everyone who plays sports needs to practice at it really hard. But he was wrong when he said you won't be able to play. If you want to play soccer and baseball, you will."

"But I can't practice."

"Why not?"

"Who am I going to practice with?" He looked over at his younger brother. "Jesse's too little to catch my fastball."

"What about me? Don't you remember who taught you to throw that fastball?"

"Justin says that his dad says, if a girl teaches you to throw, you'll throw like a girl." He gave her a lopsided smile that reminded her of his father. "Sorry, Mom, but I don't want to throw like a girl."

It was a good thing Justin's daddy wasn't there or she'd be tempted to haul off and give him a girlie punch. "I know some girls who can throw a mean strike, Todd. It shouldn't make a difference if you're a girl or a boy, honey. But I do understand your predicament, and it's a good thing I'm not a girl."

"You're not?"

"Nope, I'm a woman. And woman is spelled w-o-m-a-n. That means woooo to any m-a-n who says I throw like a girl."

Todd and Jesse both chuckled. "Really, Mom?"

"Really." She ruffled both of their heads. "Now you two get some sleep. We might have a very busy day tomorrow." She didn't feel like exploring the saloon and house any longer. What she really wanted to do was confront Justin's dad and demand to know what other foolishness he had been filling his son's head with, because it was obviously being relayed back to Todd. Wasn't her life complicated enough without worrying about what other parents were telling their children? She pressed one last kiss on each of their foreheads and crawled out of the tent.

Luke had repositioned her chair at the opposite end of the fire, away from the tent and next to his. Two cups of coffee were poured and waiting, and it looked like he had washed out the pot and packed it away for the night. By the smile twitching on his lips, it also appeared he had heard their conversation and the fact that she threw a ball like a girl. Great! Just what she needed, more taunting. More doubts. Why didn't the sissy and cootie mentality stop in elementary school?

She stomped over to her chair, picked up her coffee, and sat down. "Say one word about me throwing like a girl, and I'll sucker punch you." She kept her voice low so the boys wouldn't overhear.

Luke chuckled as he retrieved his own cup and sat down next to her. "Wouldn't dream of it." He took a sip of coffee. "Sorry for eavesdropping, but I was right there and could hear every word. I take it you're not too happy with Justin's father right now."

"I couldn't care less how Justin's dad thinks I throw. What really fries my keister is that he and his son insinuated to Todd that he wouldn't be able to play sports because he doesn't have a dad."

"From what I gather, Steven wasn't the type of father to help the boys with catching and batting practice."

Dayna stared at Luke. She honestly didn't want to bad-mouth Steven anymore, and any conversation she had concerning her late husband would surely end up that way. "Let's not talk about Steven or the past."

"If you wish." Luke took another sip of coffee and went back to contemplating the dancing flames in front of them.

Three minutes later she couldn't stand the quiet between them. He had to have heard Todd's comments about them becoming his family, but he was being polite and not bringing up that embarrassing subject. "I would like to thank you for asking about my plans for tomorrow. I'm afraid Todd and Jesse have developed a strong attachment toward you and they're both a little confused as to how to handle it."

"First off, no thanks are needed. I was out of line yesterday when I suggested hiking to Cooper's Grave. I should have run it by you first. Second, I've already figured out that they seem to have attached themselves permanently to my side. I don't mind in the least, but I can understand why you might. After all, you are their mother."

"I'm not threatened by their affection toward you, Luke. I'm quite happy that they're bonding so well to a man, but I am concerned about what happens to them when we leave here."

"What do you mean?"

"We'll go back home to Denver and you'll fly back to Washington. It might seem to them that you're deserting them. They could be hurt."

"It was never my intention to hurt the boys, or you, Dayna."

"I know." She shrugged and finished her coffee. She had said her piece. How was he to have known that the boys would perceive him as a father figure or that his kisses would awaken her dormant body? "You came here because Eileen was all upset and was fearing for the safety of her precious grandsons."

"I came here because that was what I wanted to do, Dayna. When have you ever known me to do my mother's bidding?"

He had a point there. Luke wasn't known to be a mama's boy. In fact, he was the total opposite. "Never. I've never seen you jump at your mother's endless commands."

She had always considered Grandfather Max the black sheep of the family. But the more she thought about it, the more she realized that Max had become the outcast because of his age and his helplessness, not because he wasn't true to Callahan form. Max had built the Callahan's railroad dynasty by marrying the daughter of a prominent banker while dallying with the widow of a silver mine owner. The rest, as they say, was history. Max hadn't been the black sheep, he had been the leader of the lustful flock.

Luke was the black sheep. He was the outcast who had moved east and shunned the Callahan name and his fortune in trust. In an ironic twist of fate, he was the only adult male Callahan left, until Todd and Jesse grew up. Eileen must have been desperate to call Luke, but she had no one else. Dayna was the one Eileen usually called every time some little thing upset her.

Over the last year, since Steven's death, the calls had become more frequent and petty. It had taken Dayna a while to figure Eileen out, but she had. Steven's mother was obsessed with the idea that Dayna would go out and find herself a new husband, one who would take her and the boys away from Denver. Dayna had tried explaining to Eileen that she wasn't dating, had no plans to start dating, and that the chances were she'd fly to the moon before she'd remarry. Eileen didn't believe her, and it was beyond Dayna to tell her how her precious son had managed to ruin her for any other man. Maybe Eileen had thought she was bringing a man along on this camping trip and had called for Luke to squash any budding romance.

Dayna chuckled at the thought of Eileen finding out about the kiss Luke and she had shared. Wouldn't that send the old busybody to the beauty parlor to cover up the latest gray hairs faster than a jackrabbit being chased by a fox?

"What's so funny?"

"Nothing." Dayna couldn't help chuckling again. "I'm sorry, Luke. It's this private joke that keeps running through my head."

"Care to share?"

She grinned. "Nope." Luke and she were finally getting back to being friends. She didn't want to ruin this fragile beginning by bringing up their kiss or anything else relating to last night. Today had been too much of a strain, with Luke not talking and the boys casting curious glances at them both. Todd and Jesse had picked up on the tension vibrating between them. The thought of tomorrow being a repeat of today was just too much to handle.

"Do you have any other plans," he asked, "besides exploring the buildings of the town? Is there something you or the boys might want to see or do now that I'm around to lend a helping hand?"

"Not really. I was playing it by ear, or to be more accurate, by the weather. Tomorrow's supposed to be cloudy with a chance of a sprinkle or two, so I figured we would stay pretty dry and comfortable exploring the buildings. As for the day after tomorrow, I was planning on a trip into Meeker Park. It's supposed to rain all day, and we need to pick up some more food and supplies. The laundry could stand to be tossed into a machine instead of being beaten against rocks. And since it looks like a total wash of a day, I thought we might rent a motel room for the night and enjoy the comforts of civilization."

He arched an eyebrow. "One motel room?"

It was the only gesture he ever did that reminded

her of Steven. Steven used to arch his brow like that when he was being sarcastic. Luke appeared to have another emotion in mind. "I will rent a room for the boys and me. If you wish to stay in town, I would suggest you rent your own room."

"Party pooper." A devilish gleam flashed in his eyes and a smile played across his mouth.

"So I've been told." She shook her head and chuckled. Luke seemed not in the least bit offended. "If the weather breaks by the following day, maybe we could head up to Estes Park and enter the Rocky Mountain National Park for the day. I took the boys there two years ago, but I'm sure they would enjoy a return visit. The scenery is beautiful."

"The scenery is not only beautiful, it's breathtaking."

"You've been there?"

"A couple of times many years ago."

She watched as he picked up a small stick and tossed it into the fire. The boys had quieted down a while ago and more than likely were already in dreamland. Ah . . . to be a child again.

The golden glow of the fire lit Luke's face and highlighted his dark brown hair with a deep burnished red. The shadow of his beard darkened his jaw, even though she knew he had shaved earlier. He would have appeared dangerous to anyone looking at him for the first time. She knew him better. "You didn't stay at home very much, did you?"

"Only when absolutely necessary."

She couldn't blame him. He had handled Eileen

and her obvious preference toward Steven with re- markable grace and dignity. But she was sure it must have been different when he was a little boy. He had been younger than Jesse when Steven had arrived on the scene to steal his mother's affection. She under- stood the jealousy that sometimes appeared when a new sibling was born and a child had to learn to share his parents' affection. She couldn't imagine what Luke had felt when his own mother had totally pushed him aside for the new infant.

"She was wrong, you know," she said softly.

Luke glanced over at her. "Who was wrong, and about what?"

"Your mother. She never should have pushed you away when Steve was born."

"Who said she did?"

Dayna cringed at the defensiveness in his voice, but went on anyway. Someone had to make Luke see that it was Eileen who had been in the wrong, not the little boy he had been. "No one had to say it, Luke. I know how you were raised, and I know how Steven was raised.

"There are always differences in brothers or sis- ters, but that's what makes each one of us an individ- ual. Todd and Jesse are so much alike in many ways, yet they are as different as night and day in others."

Luke picked up a small pebble and rolled it be- tween his fingers. "Do you love them both the same?"

Tears came to her eyes, and she rapidly blinked to keep Luke from knowing. The pain in his voice gripped her heart. It was the pain of a confused five-year-old boy who couldn't figure out why his mother loved his baby brother more than him. "Yes, I love them both the same."

"Would you send one away to boarding school and keep the other one home?" His gaze was riveted on the pebble rolling between his fingers.

"Never." Eileen should be horsewhipped for what she had done to Luke. "Neither of my sons would ever be sent to a boarding school." She watched the pebble move faster and faster between his long fingers.

"What happens if you remarry and your new husband wants to start a family of his own?"

"If I ever remarry, my husband would have to love Todd and Jesse as much as I do." She shook her head. "But you don't have to worry about your nephews. I have absolutely no plans to remarry, ever."

The pebble fell to the ground. "Why not?"

Dayna bit her lip and looked away. How much should she tell Luke? Maybe if she told him the truth he would stop this foolish infatuation he claimed to have for her and things could really get back to normal. Over the coming years she knew she would need some sound, reasonable, male advice concerning the boys. She wanted to be able to pick up the phone and call Luke. She had no one else.

A couple of minutes of acute embarrassment would be well worth the pain if she could count on Luke's broad shoulders later in life. She stared at the low-burning flames and softly asked, "Remember last night when you said that Steven found a person's weakness and used it against them?"

"I remember."

"Your brother had the uncanny ability to find that vulnerable point with deadly accuracy."

"Yes, he did."

Dayna worried her lower lip. She remembered what Luke had claimed was his weakness and how Steven had used it to his advantage. She didn't deserve to be anyone's weakness, most of all Luke's. "Steven knew exactly where to aim his poisonous arrows when it came to me." She shrugged, but didn't dare look at Luke. This was hard enough as it was; she didn't need to see the distaste on his face. She had seen it enough on Steven's. "Then again, maybe it was Steven who caused the vulnerability in the first place."

"What's your weakness, Dayna?"

She stared at the dancing flames and tried to picture her youth, before she had met Steven. She had dated plenty of guys throughout high school and college, but no one particular man. She had shared dozens of different kisses. Some were nice. Some were sloppy and wet. Some were sweet and warm with the promise of things to come, if she chose. Just because she never chose, didn't make her passionless.

She had felt those first stirrings of desire back then, but had chosen to wait until she married. She still believed she had been right in her thinking, but wrong in her choice. Steven had taken her youthful dreams and over time had ground them into ashes of embarrassment and doubt.

"Dayna?"

She shook her head to dislodge the mental picture of Steven's tormenting face. "Sorry." Steven wasn't all to blame. Some of it surely could be laid at her door.

"Tell me your secret, Dayna."

His voice was as gentle as the evening breeze. Luke had the voice of an angel. If she couldn't trust an angel, whom could she trust? She sighed and answered him, revealing her secret shame. "I'm frigid."

EIGHT

"You're what?" Luke asked in amazement. He obviously hadn't heard Dayna right. For a moment he would have sworn she had said she was frigid.

"I said I'm frigid." She continued staring at the fire, not at him.

He noticed the defeated set of her shoulders and wondered for the hundredth time what had really gone on between his manipulative brother and Dayna. "Who told you that nonsense?" If Dayna was frigid, he was the Pope.

"No one had to tell me, Luke. There are certain things a woman just knows."

He gave an ungentlemanly snort. "Then all I can say is you don't know jack."

She laughed softly, without humor. "Thanks, I think." She closely examined the tips of her fingers as if the subject had bored her to tears and now she wished it dropped.

There was no way he was dropping this subject. "You seem to be forgetting one thing, Dayna."

"What's that?"

"I've kissed you." He knew she did want to forget that, but he wasn't about to let her. This was his one and only chance to make Dayna see him as a man instead of the boys' uncle or Steven's brother. He wasn't going to tread lightly and do the gentlemanly thing. "And you kissed me back."

She shrugged. "Your point being?"

"You're not frigid."

"How do you know?"

"Because, my sweet little Dayna, you responded to me. Frigid people don't respond." They also didn't melt into his arms like hot silk, but he didn't think she would appreciate hearing that now.

"Okay, maybe I used the wrong word."

He watched in agony as she bit her lower lip. That single characteristic was going to drive him over the edge. All day he'd been fantasizing about those pearly whites sinking into his skin and enjoying every minute of it. He had to clear his throat twice before he could ask, "What word would you use then?"

Her head fell forward and the golden curtain of her hair hid her face from his view. She seemed to be searching for the answer. Her soft sigh filled the darkness with resignation.

"Dayna?"

"Unattractive . . . undesirable . . . uninspiring. Pick one. Any one. It doesn't really matter.

They all mean basically the same thing. I'm not the type of woman who inspires lust in a man."

He couldn't prevent the burst of laughter that erupted from him and spilled out into the night. *Dayna was the type of woman who didn't inspire lust!* What was she, crazy? He had been walking around semiaroused since he'd crossed the Mississippi River, sitting in the first-class section of a jumbo jet and heading for Colorado. Last night he hadn't been semi anything. He had gone to bed hard and throbbing and had woken up drenched in sweat and reaching for her, only to come up empty-handed. It had taken a trip at dawn down to the icy creek to make himself presentable and to make sure his jeans zipped.

"Who fed you that crap?" he asked. "Oh, no, don't tell me, let me guess. My charming brother Steven. Right?" Who else could it have been? Steven had bragged after their honeymoon that he had married the only twenty-two-year-old virgin in the state of Colorado. Since Steven's death, Dayna hadn't dated. She had shared her bed with only one man.

She glanced at him, then turned her head away. "Can't we say that I know it's true and leave it at that?"

"No, we can't."

"Why?"

"Because it isn't true, Dayna." He slipped out of his chair and knelt in front of her, taking hold of her trembling hands. "You're a very desirable woman."

He gave her a small, half hopeful smile. "Would you like me to show you how desirable?"

"It wouldn't last, Luke. Don't you see?" She tried to pull her hands out of his grip. "That's what I've been trying to tell you."

"What wouldn't last?" Was she referring to the actual physical act? It would take twenty years of loving Dayna to begin to get the burning need out of his system, if he was lucky. His gut told him he would go to his grave wanting her.

"Us . . . the desire . . ." She succeeded in pulling her hands out of his. "The sex." She bent her head and stared at her lap.

"Sex?" He reached out and raised her chin. Her sweet blue eyes were swimming with tears. Huge pools of tears. Tears big enough to drown a man. "Is that what you think this is all about, sex?"

"It doesn't matter, Luke." She gave a delicate sniffle and blinked her eyes. Still, one tear streaked down her cheek.

He captured the drop with the tip of his thumb. "That's where you're wrong, Dayna. It matters very much." A second tear slid down her cheek and he swiped it away too. "If all I wanted was sex, I could get that from any number of women."

"So what do you want from me then?"

She looked so lost and confused, he could do nothing but give her the truth. "I want to make love *with* you, Dayna."

"But don't you see, you can't."

Tears were now streaking down her face faster

than he could catch them. It tore at his heart that she was refusing him, but her obvious distress pained him more. "Okay, Dayna. If that's your wish, I'll honor it. I've never forced myself on a woman before and I'll be damned if I start now."

She shook her head and wiped her tears away with the back of her hand. "It has nothing to do with what I wish, Luke."

"Then what does it have to do with?"

"Me." She closed her eyes and whispered, "I can't please a man in bed."

Luke froze at her softly spoken confession. Dayna thought she couldn't please a man in bed? It was insane. It was totally untrue. But judging by the heat flooding her face, the droop of her shoulders, the trembling of her fingers, he would have to say she believed it.

He closed his eyes and sat back, trying to gather his perplexed thoughts. What had Steven done to her? It was the only explanation. Steven had to be at the root of it all.

For a moment he almost gave up. Steven had won. Even beyond the grave Steven was denying him something he wanted very dearly—Dayna's love. Once again Steven had gotten what Luke wanted, only to toss it away. All his life, Steven would damage or even destroy whatever he had obtained, then cast it aside and leave the broken pieces for his older brother to cry over.

A 1914 Stutz Bearcat, Grandfather Max's pride and joy, was supposed to have been willed to Luke.

When Steven was nineteen he had broken into the garage and taken the mint-condition car for a joyride. The Bearcat had ended up at the bottom of a ravine in a burning mass of rumble, while Steven had only sustained a few minor injuries. That was only one of many things Luke had wanted that Steven had stolen. The greatest loss, the one that still grieved him, was their mother's affection.

Over the years, he had learned to hide his feelings and desires from Steven. He hadn't succeeded with Dayna. Steven had known his older brother desired his wife and had tried to destroy Dayna as surely as he had pushed the Bearcat over the side of the road. Steven's last act of petty revenge had been taken out on an innocent woman.

Luke couldn't allow that to happen. Steven wasn't going to win this last round. Somehow, some way, he was going to make Dayna see what a desirable woman she was. He might not be able to win her love, but he would give her the gift of passion.

He took her hands in his and stood up, gently pulling her out of the chair. They were standing so close, he could smell the wild berry fragrance of her shampoo. "A man can only be pleased if he wants to, Dayna." He wiped the last of the moisture from her face. "Steven didn't want to be pleased. Nothing you could have done would have changed that."

"How do you know?"

"I knew my brother." He couldn't tell her she had been the pawn in Steven's revenge. He couldn't tell the woman he had grown to love that he was the reason behind the cruel words Steven must have used against her. He traced the lush curve of her lower lip and smoothed the rough spot where her teeth had bit. "You're a very desirable woman, Dayna." He could feel the swelling in his jeans and silently cursed his own weakness. He wanted to show her how appealing she was, not scare her with his inability to control his own body.

"I'm clumsy and awkward." Her gaze never left his.

He groaned as her tongue moistened the path his finger had just taken. "I've never known you to be either. You once told me you suffered through five years of ballet lessons because of your mother."

She gave a ghost of a smile. "There are some things ballet class never taught."

He smiled back. "I should hope so." Lord, how he wanted to kiss her again. He needed to taste her again. "Can I kiss you?"

Her expression revealed confusion and a spark of some emotion he couldn't identify. He nearly died when her gaze zeroed in on his mouth and something akin to hunger leaped in her eyes. She swallowed. "I don't know, Luke."

"Don't let him win. Prove to yourself you're a passionate woman." He brushed strands of her hair behind her ear. "Prove to yourself that you can make a man want you."

"I won't sleep with you to prove Steven wrong."

"I'm not asking you to, Dayna. I'm asking you to kiss me. That's all. Nothing more."

"Nothing?"

"Nothing more than you're willing to give."

"What if all I want is a kiss?"

"Then that's all I'm willing to take." He cupped her cheek and smiled at the way she leaned into his hand.

She chewed on her lower lip for a moment. "And if I want more?"

"I won't sleep with you to prove my brother was wrong, Dayna. I already know he was wrong." He smoothed her lower lip with his thumb. "But I will allow you to kiss me to prove it to yourself. There's no way I can hide my desire from you."

"You won't sleep with me?" The confusion and self-doubt were back in her eyes and voice.

"I didn't say that. I said I won't sleep with you to prove Steven wrong." He slid his hand around to the back of her head and pulled her closer. "When we make love it will be because we both want to and it will have absolutely nothing to do with Steven or the past." He wanted to tell her it would have everything to do with the future, but she wasn't ready to hear that.

She raised her mouth to his. "When? Not *if*?"

He chuckled and brushed his mouth against hers. "So sue me, I'm an optimist."

Her arms wrapped around his neck. "I love an optimist." She pressed her mouth against his and matched his heat.

❖⎯⎯❖

Dayna listened as the wooden steps groaned precariously under her feet. "Are you sure it's safe, Luke?"

What was she asking him for? she asked herself with wry humor. Last night she had been anything but safe. Luke had taken her into his arms and she had discovered a whole new meaning to the word desire. She had wanted Luke more than she had wanted to breathe, but she was still afraid of failing. Too many years of ridicule had left her with nothing but self-doubt. Thanks to the dozen or so heated kisses she had shared with Luke by the fire, he had come a long way in stripping some of that doubt away. He hadn't pressured her, and he had allowed her to set the pace and call a halt when she felt things were becoming out of control.

Luke turned around and smiled at her. "Just stay away from the banister and you should be fine."

There was something different about his smile this morning, she mused. Luke's smile had always had the power to capture her attention. But this morning it was dazzling. It was personal. It spoke of passion-filled kisses and the promise of more to come. And it was directed right at her.

Luke glanced at Todd and Jesse behind her. "You both remember the rules? Don't touch what's remaining of the railing, stay within my sight, no running, and stay out of the very back room. The weather has done a lot of damage in there, and I don't trust the floorboards."

Both boys had the same expression they wore

Christmas morning as they surveyed the pile of brightly wrapped presents beneath the tree. Luke was giving them Christmas morning in the middle of July, for what could be more exciting than the possibility of exploring forbidden territory? The first day they had arrived at Aces High they both had begged, pleaded, and done everything short of complete disobedience to get their mother to allow them to search the second floor of the house or saloon. She had refused even to venture up there to see if it was safe. Visions of herself falling through a rotted floorboard and stranding all three of them out in the middle of nowhere were enough to make her one very cautious camper.

Luke was another story. He was strong and capable, and she was there if he got into any trouble. His examination of the floors, ceiling, and main structure had been cautious and thorough. He wouldn't allow anything to happen to himself, the boys, or to her. She trusted his judgment. It was a strange and unsettling feeling to admit it to herself. She trusted Luke with her sons' lives when she wouldn't have trusted their own father.

She watched as Luke ruffled Jesse's hair as they shared some private joke, more than likely about gunslingers. Jesse and Todd were becoming tired of her stories of prospectors and gold mining, and had pumped Luke for everything he knew or had heard about the notorious Old West. Outlaws held more appeal than white-whiskered old men and their mules. The vicious gun fights of the Old West were commonplace enough, but she would rather dwell on less violent aspects of the past.

The hallway upstairs was covered in dust, cobwebs, and debris she wasn't curious enough to examine too closely. There were a total of six rooms leading off the narrow hall. Out of the six, only two still had doors hanging haphazardly from the jambs.

Luke pointed to the farthest opening. "That's the room you're not allowed in."

Both boys eyed the opening with great interest. "Can we at least look into it?" Todd asked.

"Sure." Luke shrugged and glanced over their heads at her. "The hallway's safe enough. But there's nothing to see."

Todd and Jesse followed Luke to the doorway and both eagerly peered inside. Neither boy said a word but their disappointment was clearly etched on their faces. "I warned you there was nothing to see," Luke said.

Dayna surveyed the nine-by-nine room with mild curiosity. There was one window, minus the glass and most of its frame. The floor was stained dark and appeared rotted from the rain and the snow having blown in through the window. She wouldn't have trusted the floorboards either. At one time there must have been paint on the walls, but now it was impossible to identify what color it had been. A rusty iron bed frame lay crumbled in the middle of the floor and what appeared to be a bird's nest had been constructed above a peg board running the length of one wall.

"Gee, and I thought my room was small," Jesse said.

"Notice how they didn't have closets," Dayna added. "They hung what little clothing they possessed on the pegs, or sometimes they owned a wardrobe."

"What's that?" asked Todd. He had turned away from the room and was scanning the other doorways.

"It's a cabinet containing some shelves, a rod to hang clothes on, and perhaps some drawers. Kind of like a portable closet. This room was probably rented to people who needed a place to stay for the night."

"Oh. Can I pick the first room we can go in?" Todd asked, totally uninterested in how the Old West had hung their clothes.

So much for her lesson concerning old-time furniture. "Sure. You pick the next room and then Jesse gets a turn."

Todd raced to the opposite end of the hallway with Jesse in tow. Luke and Dayna hurried after them. "Wait for us," she called, laughing. She didn't think she had ever seen the boys so excited about anything.

"They'll be fine," Luke said, and grabbed her hand.

The warmth of his hand raced up her arm and surrounded her heart. Even as the temperature climbed outside, it had felt cool inside the run-down saloon. Luke's nearness raised the temperature till she thought she was overdressed wearing black shorts, old sneakers, and a T-shirt that read "If you can read this shirt, thank a teacher." She had pulled her hair back into a ponytail in preparation for the heat that would surely come that afternoon.

Luke was dressed in a pair of faded jeans, tough-looking hiking boots, and a cotton shirt that gave new meaning to the term "fabric of our lives." She would dearly love to be that fabric and cling to his chest for the day.

"Aren't you going to be warm in those long pants and boots?" she asked.

He glanced at the boys, who had chosen a room and were waiting for them to catch up. He pulled her to a halt and whispered, "Are you trying to get me out of my pants?"

A fiery blush swept up her cheeks.

"Come on, you two," Todd called. "I see stuff."

Luke chuckled. "You're going to love this room," he told her, and grinned wickedly. "I can't wait to see how you explain it to the boys."

She grabbed his hand as he started to walk away. "Why? What's in there?"

"Mom!" Todd and Jesse cried in unison. Somewhere in the building a bird squawked in protest of the loud noise, and the scurrying of tiny feet could be heard throughout the building.

"Come on," Luke teased as he pulled her toward the boys. "The Land Barons are getting restless."

She reluctantly followed. One look into the room and she knew exactly what Luke had been referring to. The room had obviously belonged to one of the "ladies" of the establishment. The walls had been papered with a red fabric that might have been silk. Now it was just tattered scraps. The glass from the doors leading to the balcony was gone, but the overhang on the roof had protected the room from the majority of the weather. Wisps of what had once been lace curtains still hung from the doors.

The boys walked into the room as if entering a shrine. Dayna watched them as they started to examine the contents of the room. They headed immediately for the largest piece of furniture. "That's a wardrobe," she said, "like I told you about." The double doors were missing and only one shelf was left inside. It looked as if the whole thing would crumble into dust if she blew on it. "Don't touch it."

"Your mother's right, boys," Luke said. "It would probably collapse into toothpicks. Just look inside." He walked over to the wardrobe and stood beside her.

Dayna watched as the boys turned away, unimpressed. She spied a scrap of lace tucked into the corner and gently, without touching the wood, picked it up. The fragile material fell apart in her fingers.

"What was it?" asked Todd.

"It looked like it might have been the edge of a hankie or perhaps a collar to a dress." There were probably a dozen different articles of clothing a "soiled dove" could have owned that contained lace, but she wasn't about to broaden her sons' education in that direction. Luke was another story. He had grinned as she passed the lace off as part of a hankie or a collar. He knew.

"Wow, Mom. Look at the bed," Jesse said.

Dayna turned her attention to what was left of the iron and brass bed. At one time the frame must have been gorgeous, but now it was beyond repair. She reached out and touched the corroded iron and pitted brass headboard that was leaning against the wall. The footboard had crumbled to the floor. Someone had taken a lot of trouble to haul the once-fancy head- and footboard all the way to the middle of the Rockies. "It must have been beautiful at one time."

The remnants of a table lay next to the bed. Under the dust, dirt, and debris on the floor appeared to be what had once been a rug. A dressing table with a blackened mirror stood against the far wall. Under the decades of dust sat a woman's prized possessions: a comb and brush set, what appeared to be a perfume bottle, and other baubles. Trinkets of a time forgotten. It was a sad testimony to all that remained of the woman who had lived and worked in this room.

Dayna had seen the ghostly reminders of the past all over the town, but nothing spoke of the people as clearly as this long-forgotten room. Aces High had had its share of prospectors, card sharks, and the occasional outlaw, if Luke's stories could be believed, and now she could add a dance hall girl to the list of residents. There were still four other rooms to explore, so maybe there had been more than one prostitute, but somehow it didn't matter. This was the room that spoke of it all. This was where her heart connected with the past. Was the woman who had lived in this room, servicing the patrons below, happy? What kind of life had she lived? And what sad circumstances had driven her to this profession?

"Dayna?" Luke called.

She shook her head to dislodge the past. "I'm sorry, Luke. Did you say something?"

"You seemed a million miles away."

"No." She studied the top of the dresser. "Just a hundred years." She lightly blew up a cloud of dust to get a better look. The brush and comb were cracked and crumbling. The tattered remains of a bureau scarf were visible under the brush. The only item on the dresser that wasn't reverting to dust was a small pink glass ball with a flat bottom, about three inches in diameter. She reached for the ball and gently picked it up. As carefully as she could she wiped the fragile bauble on the hem of her T-shirt. The pink glass sparkled in the light.

"What is it, Mom?" asked Todd, as he and Jesse came over to see what she had found.

"It's a piece of glass."

"Does it have anything inside it?" Todd asked, trying to get a better look.

"No, it's just solid glass by the feel of it." She held it up to the light coming in through the doors and watched as the sunbeams streamed through the glass, turning everything pink. The imperfections in the glass, of which there were many, shot prisms against the wall.

"Hey, neat," Jesse said.

"It's only girl's stuff," complained Todd, bored with the simple trick of light. "Let's go to the next room."

Dayna was still fascinated with the glass ball and what it must have meant to the woman who lived in this room. Something as simple as a piece of glass had obviously been very special to the woman for her to have placed it with all her other treasures.

Todd and Jesse were standing by the doorway waiting for her when the noise came. Everyone froze as the sound of heavy footsteps crossing the saloon below reached their ears.

Jesse hurried to his mother's side, with Todd right behind him. "It's a ghost," Jesse whispered.

"No, it's not." Dayna pulled her sons close. There were no such things as ghosts. Whoever was heading for the stairs was real, but they hadn't heard a car pull into town. "Maybe it's a hiker."

Luke motioned Dayna and her sons farther back into the room as the footsteps started to climb the stairs. He leaned in close and whispered, "Don't go out onto the balcony. It's not safe."

She understood exactly what he was saying. They were trapped in this room with nowhere to hide. If this were indeed the Old West, Luke would have a six-shooter strapped to his thigh. As it was they were defenseless against the approaching intruder. Dayna gave the boys a reassuring smile and nonchalantly moved them behind her as the footsteps drew nearer.

Both boys peered around her, their eye-bulging gazes glued to the doorway.

Luke stepped in front of Dayna and faced the door. Short of ripping off one of the dresser's legs, there wasn't a single item in the room he could use as a weapon.

Dayna's fingers tightened around the glass ball in her hand. As far as weapons went, it wasn't much, but it was all she had. A dark shadow crossed the doorway, then the man appeared.

Dayna looked around Luke and blinked in surprise. Both of her sons sucked in their breath at the sight of the man standing in the doorway. He appeared to be around seventy years old and had whiter hair and a longer beard than Santa. His clothes were dusty, three sizes too big, and so far out-of-date it would take a history book to place them. His face was tanned and toughened by decades of sun and the elements. He didn't look too pleased to find them there.

He glanced around the room, then glared at all four of them. His deep voice thundered, startling everyone. "What in the hell are you doing in Annie's room?"

NINE

"Annie's room," Dayna whispered. She glanced down at the glass ball clutched in her fist and slowly relaxed her fingers. This was Annie's trinket.

"Who's Annie?" Luke asked.

"Who are you folks and what are you doing in Prosperity?" The old man eyed the glass bauble in Dayna's hand and glared at her.

"The town's name was changed to Aces High nearly seventy years ago," Luke said. He gestured to Todd and Jesse, who were still speechless and hiding behind their mother. "This is Todd and Jesse Callahan, the owners of this saloon and the rest of the town."

The old man eyed the boys with great interest. "You be Max's grandchildren?"

"Great-grandchildren, sir," Todd whispered as he stepped out from behind Dayna.

"You knew my grandfather?" Luke asked.

The old man turned his gaze on Luke. "Let's say I heard about him. Didn't he pass over just a couple of months ago?"

"Pass over?"

"Kissed the dust. Cashed in his chips. Crossed the great divide. You know, died." He glanced at Todd and Jesse and managed a small smile. "No disrespect to your great-grandpa, boys."

"It's okay," replied Todd.

"Grandpa Max said he'd be pushing up daisies come spring," Jesse added importantly.

The old man burst out laughing. "You're Max's kin all right. The apple doesn't fall far from the tree."

"Where did you say you heard of my grandfather?" Luke asked. He relaxed his stance but continued to eye the stranger cautiously.

"Didn't, sonny." He winked at the boys, and Dayna noticed how only one of his piercing blue eyes moved. The other one appeared to be glass.

Luke held out his hand. "I'm Luke Callahan, and this is Dayna."

The old man rubbed his chin full of whiskers and studied Luke's outstretched hand. He didn't reach for the hand. "Right nice family you have there, Luke. Max did himself proud."

Luke lowered his hand, but didn't correct the man on his assumption that Dayna and the boys were his. "Who might you be," he asked, "and how did you get to Aces High? We didn't hear any cars approach."

"Folks around here call me Pete, and I got here the same way I always do, me and Freckles walked." He glanced back at the boys. "Max changed the name to Aces High?"

"Yes, sir," Jesse said. "Grandpa said he won it in a poker game from a prospector named One-eyed Pete. He had a pair of aces to Pete's pair of kings." Jesse's eyes widened like huge saucers. "Your name is Pete too!"

"So it is, son. So it is." Pete chuckled loudly. "Max told you he won the town with aces high?"

Jesse nodded.

"What if I were to tell you he won it with a pair of fives over a pair of lousy fours?"

Dayna laughed to herself. Leave it to Max to name a town after an untruth. The old Callahan charm had struck again. Then she frowned at the old man. "How would you know what cards he held and what cards he beat?" It seemed a mighty big coincidence, too, that this prospector and the one Max had won the town from were both named Pete. The coincidence doubled if you added the fact that both men owned mules named Freckles.

Pete grinned and stepped farther into the room. "One hears things."

"What kind of things?" she asked, willing herself not to step back. She wasn't physically afraid of Pete. The man had to be seventy if he was a day. Luke could subdue him easily enough. Considering his gnarled hands, stooped shoulders, and the lack of vision out of one eye, she would say she could take him herself if push came to shove. But she wasn't worried about a physical confrontation with Pete. There was something strange about the old man. Something that didn't sit just right.

"At my age," Pete answered, "a man's heard all kinds of things." He glanced at the glass ball still in her hand. "What are you doing with Annie's prized possession?"

She looked at the sphere. "How do you know it was Annie's?"

"It was sitting in her room, wasn't it?" He nodded in the direction of the dresser and gazed knowingly at the dust-free spot where the ball had been sitting.

"How would you know whose room this was?" Luke asked. "All records indicate that this town was deserted sometime in 1890. You weren't even born yet."

"Records have been known to be wrong."

Dayna rubbed her finger over the shimmering glass. "Was Annie happy?" She didn't doubt Pete for one minute. Someone named Annie would surely keep this trinket as a prized possession.

"As much as her circumstances allowed, ma'am." He glanced at the orb. "Heard tell that there glass came all the way from Philadelphia."

His pronunciation of Philadelphia was off and the way he said the name made it sound like the city was on the other side of the earth, not just a couple of hours away by plane.

"Do you know how Annie got it?" Dayna asked.

"Rumor was her one true love gave it to her."
Pete eyed her curiously. "You like it?"

"It's beautiful." In reality she had seen countless
more exquisite works of arts. Crystals that captured
a thousand lights. Perfect glass balls containing everything from rose petals to snowmen and glistening
snowflakes. In a discount department store, Annie's
ball would be placed in a bin with a slashed price
sticker. But there was something so simple and cap-
tivating about the pale pink glass, it fascinated her.

"Why don't you keep it." Pete said. "Annie
wouldn't have liked to see it sit here for eternity
collecting dust. I think she would like you to have
it."

"You seem to know a lot about Annie," Luke said
as he motioned the boys out the door.

Pete's smile crinkled up his leathery face. "One
does hear stories." He glanced at the boys. "How
about I take you guys for a tour of the saloon? If you
think I know a lot about a pretty little dove named
Annie, you should hear what I know about saloons."

Both boys enthusiastically nodded their heads.
"Can we, Mom?" asked Todd.

"Can we, please?" Jesse added.

She glanced at Luke, who shrugged. "I don't see
why not. I would love to learn more about the saloon from an expert." She grinned at Pete, who
grinned back.

"That's me, ma'am. The expert in salooning,
panning for gold, and Annie." He stepped briskly

into the hall. "Come on, boys, I'll tell you everything I know about Prosperity."

"It's Aces High," said Jesse.

"It was Prosperity when it sprang from the dust
and it will be Prosperity when it returns," grumbled
Pete. He eased his complaint with a soft, sad
chuckle. "At least in my mind it will be."

Todd stopped outside a doorway to one of the
bedrooms they hadn't explored yet. "Hey, Pete, do
you know anything about outlaws?"

Pete cackled with glee. "Outlaws, you say." He
winked at Dayna as they all entered the bedroom to
begin his tour. "Now there's a subject I just might
be able to help you out with."

Four hours later Dayna stood beside Luke and
the boys and watched as Pete and his mule slowly
disappeared into the trees. The entire morning and
early afternoon had been a wondrous experience for
them all. Pete had been a fountain of information,
and the stories he told were so real, one might think
he'd actually lived in Prosperity during its prime.

Of course, that was impossible. Prosperity had
died over a hundred years ago. No one was alive
who had witnessed its rise or fall. So how had Pete
known about Annie, or Clem the bartender, or the
Reynolds family who had lived in the fancy house?
He had probably made it all up, Dayna decided, adding names to make the stories more enjoyable for
the boys. Whoever he was, he was a gold mine of

information. She had even invited him to visit the school where she taught in Denver to tell his stories. After he had stopped laughing, he'd politely declined her offer, saying something about being in Denver once before and it was too crowded for him, what with the railroad and such.

Dayna had thought it was a peculiar way of describing a city the size of Denver, but now as she watched the trees swallow Pete and his mule, she wasn't too sure. Pete appeared to have stepped out of the past into the present day. His clothes were not only threadbare, they were ancient. Half the equipment strapped across Freckles's back belonged in a museum. Pete appeared not to own one item that would place him within the twentieth century.

"Mom?"

"Yes, Todd?"

"Could that have been the same prospector Grandpa Max won the town from?"

"No, son. Max won the town nearly seventy years ago. Pete looked about seventy himself, so that would mean he was just a baby at the time."

"But he has a mule named Freckles."

"He probably heard the stories about the first Pete and decided it would be neat to have a mule named Freckles too."

"He seemed to know a whole bunch about Aces High," added Jesse.

"A lot of people," Luke said, "really get into the history of places and the people who lived there. Pete obviously likes to get into the role of being a prospector. Back in Virginia a lot of men dress up like Union or Confederate soldiers and do reenactments of the Civil War. It's not unusual to bump into Grant or Lee during the height of the tourist season."

Dayna couldn't imagine anyone getting into the role so much, he'd go out and purchase a mule, then wander through the Rockies for the sheer joy of it. Pete had mentioned that he was searching for "his way." His way to what he hadn't bothered to explain. He had just smiled secretly and changed the subject. Maybe he meant he was searching for that elusive mother lode.

"But he only had one eye," whispered Jesse. "The other one didn't work."

"Well, that's true," Dayna said. How was she going to explain this to the boys when she herself didn't fully understand. "Pete has a glass eye. Maybe that, along with his age and long hair and beard, made him the perfect choice to act out the role of the old prospector." She turned around and headed everyone back to camp. A reassuring smile lit her face. "I bet his real name isn't even Pete. It's probably Horace, or Wilbur, or even Bob."

Both boys laughed and ran ahead of her and Luke, shouting men's names, each one more ridiculous than the one before. Dayna glanced up at the darkening skies. The weather was going to break sooner than the radio had predicted. They were in for a rough night.

"Do you think they bought it?" Luke asked.

"Bought what?" She definitely didn't like the looks of the dark, ominous clouds gathering toward the west.

"The nice, tidy, and far-fetched explanation of Pete, the one-eyed prospector."

"Why was it far-fetched?" She knew she had pushed more than the envelope coming up with that last explanation, but it still beat what had been playing through her mind. You just didn't go around telling six- and eight-year-olds about time warps.

"If Pete was just some history buff dressed for the part," Luke said, "It leaves a couple of very interesting questions."

"Like?"

"Who was he supposed to be reenacting for? No one knew we would be at Aces High. As far as I know there are no Old West reenactments out here with crusty old prospectors wandering the mountains."

"So what are you suggesting? That Pete was a ghost?" Let him be the first to admit it. She was keeping her mouth closed on that subject.

"I don't believe in ghosts." He reached out and held her hand.

"Neither do I." She squeezed his strong, warm fingers and immediately felt safer. "He didn't look or feel like a ghost."

"You touched him?"

A frown pulled at her brow. "Come to think of it, I didn't. He seemed to move away as soon as one of us got too close. He didn't even shake your hand."

"I noticed." Luke pulled her closer and looked ahead toward the boys, then back to where Pete had gone. "I also noticed he didn't eat any of the lunch you fixed him. He just pushed the food around on his plate, then dumped it into the ashes of our camp-fire when he thought no one was looking."

"That's strange." She pressed closer to Luke.

"Relax." He brushed the top of her head with his mouth. "I also didn't see through him or notice that he walked through any walls."

She chuckled at her overactive imagination. There were no such things as ghosts. "It must be the approaching storm making me edgy."

Luke glanced up at the sky and frowned. "I think we're in for a heavy downpour."

"Maybe we should think about driving into Meeker Park and grabbing rooms for the night."

"If we pack up now, we could make it by dinner-time. My treat."

She pushed herself away from him and smiled. "What's the matter? Getting tired of canned spa-ghetti, canned stew, and burnt marshmallows?"

"A thick juicy steak wouldn't go unappreciated right about now."

Dayna gave her scalp a delicate little scratch. "Neither would a shower."

Luke chuckled and pulled her in the direction of the camp. "Then what are we waiting for?"

Dayna stood under the hot water and rinsed her hair for the third time. The shower was the closest thing to heaven she'd felt all week, except for Luke's kisses. Thoughts of Luke and his steamy kisses sent her body into overload. What was she going to do about him? What could she do? There was no escaping the inevitable. She was in love with him.

Three hours ago they had been sitting in a steak house in the middle of Meeker Park when it hit her. She loved Luke Callahan. He had been sitting across from her, devouring an inch-thick steak, teasing the boys about their puny quarter pound cheeseburgers, and laughing at her chicken breast, when she'd realized she was in love. There was no other explanation for her feelings toward him. Luke had stolen her heart and captured her body with secret desires. She wanted to experience the passion his kisses promised, but she was afraid.

Too many taunts and too many nights of scorn from Steven had made her doubt herself as a woman. Luke was changing all that. He was showing her that she could feel desire and was capable of arousing it in him. Luke wanted her. She could feel it in the way his muscles trembled beneath her fingertips. She could hear it in his harsh breathing and the thickening of his arousal whenever they kissed. She could see it in his eyes. Luke Callahan's deep brown eyes held nothing but hunger when they looked at her, and she felt his need clean down to her toes. She responded to that need with one of her own. A need more powerful than anything she had experienced in life.

But still she might fail.

Angrily she shut off the water. Why was she so afraid of failing? Because of Steven. Because she didn't want to see the same ridicule in Luke's eyes as she'd witnessed in Steven's. Because in Luke's eyes it would hurt so much more.

She wrapped a towel around her hair and stepped out of the tub. The possibility of resurrecting all the self-doubt and uncertainties from years past pulled heavily on her mind. She thought she had been through that and had conquered her fears. Obviously, she hadn't. She had overcome her failing at marriage by asking Steven to leave and by filing for divorce, but she had erected barriers around herself to keep herself safe from being hurt by any other men. Now she had to decide if she was strong enough to take a risk on Luke, or was she going to continue to hide from life? Was love worth the risk?

Taut with nervous energy, she rubbed her hair with the towel. She hadn't packed a hair dryer for the camping trip. She also hadn't packed any nightgowns, makeup, or a bathrobe. The only pajamas she had was an oversize T-shirt with Tweety Bird printed on the front and a pair of men's plaid boxers. Sexy, it wasn't. But it modestly covered her and was comfortable to sleep in.

She stared into the steam-clouded mirror and

frowned. She was tired of being modestly covered, and being comfortable had become just too darn . . . comfortable. Her fingers quivering, she wiped some of the condensation from the mirror and studied her face. It was the same face that had stared back at her every morning for the past thirty-one years. It was the face of a stranger.

Where was the smile that had been permanently attached during her childhood? Her father had called her Dimples when she was a little girl. Now she feared the dimples had vanished from lack of use, just as her father was gone. Lord, how she missed her parents. Maybe if they hadn't been killed so soon after her wedding, she wouldn't have felt the self-destructive need to stay with Steven and make it work. Steven had been her family and she had clung to him with everything she had. Until Todd and then Jesse had made their appearances, her life with Steven hadn't been that horrible. Most of their problems had started after the boys were born.

She picked up her face moisturizer and applied a liberal amount. Tiny wrinkles were beginning to make their presence known at the corners of her eyes. She didn't panic over the crinkles, nor was she going to rush out to make an appointment with a plastic surgeon. Age happened. But she didn't want to age alone.

Todd and Jesse would be growing up before she knew it and starting lives of their own. It was the way of the world and she could accept that. What she didn't want to accept was that she'd be facing the rest of her life alone. There would only be one coffee cup in the sink. One toothbrush hanging in the bathroom. One side of the bed slept in. She wouldn't have anyone to share the joys or the sorrows of life with. She would never hold the daughter she had always dreamed about in her arms. All because she was afraid to believe what Luke's kisses promised.

She wasn't naive enough to think that just because they made love, life would be perfect. Luke never mentioned the future. He lived two thousand miles away and had a life back east. Her life was here in Colorado. Luke hadn't said that he loved her, only that he desired her. She was smart enough to know the difference and not to expect the impossible. There would be no daughter, no second toothbrush, no second coffee cup in her sink. But they did have one more week together. Could she live with herself and her regrets if she allowed Luke to fly back out of her life without experiencing his touch? Without knowing for sure if she would fail?

Dayna picked up her hairbrush and left the bathroom. Jesse was already asleep, and Todd was having a hard time keeping his eyes open. The television was softly droning about luxury cars and beer. "Is the show over?"

"Just about." Todd yawned.

She glanced at the slightly ajar door that connected their room with Luke's. "Where's Uncle Luke?"

"He said he was going to take a shower." Todd's

eyes closed as the characters on the sitcom he'd been watching pitched their closing joke, and the credits started to roll.

Dayna sat down on one of the chairs in front of the heater, which was taking the chill and dampness from the room, and brushed her wet hair. She could hear the shower running in Luke's room, and her mind started to play the "What If?" game. What if they were alone in his room? What if she was sitting on his bed when he stepped out of the bathroom? What if she went and joined him in the shower? What if she became clumsy and awkward and Luke pushed her away?

The doubts were back, but so was her determination to find out once and for all. Was she to blame, or was Luke right in his assumption that it had to have been Steven's fault?

She glanced at Todd and Jesse. Both were fast asleep. With the days they'd been having, and the comfort of a soft bed and pile of blankets, both would stay that way till long past dawn. The night was hers to do with as she pleased. She glanced at the connecting door and chewed her lower lip.

Thirty seconds later, her mind was made up. She clicked off the television, tucked her sons in tighter, and turned off all the lights except the one in the bathroom. She partially closed the bathroom door, bathing the room in a soft glow so the boys wouldn't be afraid if they did wake up.

Luke's shower stopped just as she walked through the connecting door and locked it. She glanced around his room. It was identical to hers except the two double beds didn't appear to have been jumped on. Luke's duffel bag was opened on the far bed, and a mound of dirty laundry was piled semi-neatly on the floor. They had agreed earlier that dinner and showers were more important than clean laundry. Tomorrow they would find a laundromat.

The sounds of Luke moving around in the bathroom caused her to tremble with fear and desire. Both emotions were playing havoc with her nerves, but she wasn't leaving. At least not until she knew for sure. She glanced around the room and wondered what she was supposed to do now. Reclining seductively across his bed wearing a Tweety Bird nightshirt was too ludicrous to contemplate. Turning on the television seemed unwise. Luke might come out of the bathroom and think she had just come into his room to watch TV so she wouldn't wake the boys. Then she would have to explain why she was in his room. Explaining what she wanted was out, she would never have the courage. Luke had better open the door and put two and two together and come up with the right answer himself.

Not knowing what to do, she turned off all but one light and walked over to the window. She cracked the blinds. The view from the door of the motel rooms was the neon-lit parking lot. The view from the window was well worth the price of the room. The majestic Rockies rose to the heavens and pierced the night sky. They appeared close enough to touch, yet she knew they were miles away.

She heard the bathroom door open, but didn't turn around. The slight sound of his movement across the room made her shiver.

"Turn around, Dayna."

She bit her lip and slowly turned. Luke stood three feet away. His hair was damp and tousled from his shower. The clean lines of his jaw spoke of his recent shaving. His chest and feet were bare. The only article of clothing he was wearing was a pair of navy sweatpants, loosely tied so they drooped low on his hips. Her curious gaze savored every damp curl covering his chest. Those twisting curls tapered off, to arrow their way down his flat stomach, only to flare out again and disappear into the band of his sweats. His muscles seemed to tighten and twitch beneath her gaze.

"Are you sure, Dayna?"

No, she was not sure. She had never felt like this before. She was in love with a man who didn't love her back. Desire her, yes. Felt some strange sense of responsibility for her, yes. Really love her? She doubted it. But what else could she do? She could pack up the boys, go back to Denver, and live with the regrets. She'd been living with regrets for years, and she wasn't about to add to them. She took a step closer to Luke and lightly stroked his chest. He shuddered beneath her touch. "Yes, I'm sure."

He groaned something that sounded like a

prayer and pulled her into his arms. His mouth was all hunger and heat as it captured hers.

She wrapped her arms around his neck and pressed herself against his chest. His heat melted the past into distant memories. There was only the here and now. She parted her lips and met Luke's tongue stroke for stroke, their mouths mating.

His hands explored and tantalized until she couldn't stand it any longer. She needed Luke. She needed him now. Her plea was a soft moan. Her fingers trembled as she plucked at the tie of his sweatpants. "Now, Luke." She sucked in a much needed breath. "Please."

He lifted his mouth from her throat. "We have to slow down, love."

She shook her head as the knot finally gave. "Later. We'll slow down later." Something deliciously sinful was happening to her body and she didn't want it to end. She wanted Luke deep inside her to make the ache go away. With eager fingers she pushed the cotton material over his hips and stroked the hard muscular curve of his buttocks.

Luke yanked her T-shirt over her head, and his mouth captured a hard nipple.

The need deep inside her pulsed with every tugging motion of his mouth. She wanted more. She arched her hips and gloried in the feel of his arousal pressing against the junction of her thighs. The only barrier between them was a pair of faded boxer shorts. She wanted that barrier gone. She wanted to get on with her life, and Luke was her life.

The heat from his fingers scorched her back, her stomach, her breasts. She could feel his breath against her nipple. Her fingers sank into his thick hair and held him closer. The dewy moisture coating the tip of her breast was matched by the gathering wetness between her thighs.

Her hands became urgent upon his body. She was about to come apart in his arms, and she wanted him with her every step of the way. Her fingers raced up his thigh to caress his manhood.

He backed away from her touch and said hoarsely, "I can't last."

"I don't want you to." She pushed down the boxers and kicked them aside before backing up to the bed. She studied his face, looking for any signs of distaste or boredom. The only thing she could detect was desire, need, and an emotion she couldn't identify but prayed was love. "Make love to me, Luke."

He smiled and walked toward her. "Try stopping me now."

She shyly matched his smile. In the morning she probably would bury her face in mortification at her actions tonight. But she wouldn't regret them. "I wouldn't dream of it."

Luke walked to the other bed, picked up his wallet, and removed something. He tossed the red foil package onto the nightstand before advancing on her with a wicked grin. "I used to dream of you like this." His gaze caressed her naked body, leaving no doubt what he had been dreaming about.

She glanced at the bed behind her. "Sometimes the reality doesn't live up to the dreams."

He stepped closer and tenderly cupped her chin, forcing her to look at him. "And sometimes, the reality surpasses them." He brushed her mouth with his. "I love you, Dayna. I would never hurt you."

She threw herself into his arms and captured his words with her hungry mouth. He loved her! Everything was going to work out. Life was perfect. Luke loved her.

She felt the softness of the mattress against her back. His kisses ignited a wildfire in her body. Somewhere in the vortex of desire she knew he reached for the protection he had tossed onto the nightstand. And then he was there. Deep inside her, touching her soul, chanting her name.

Worrying about being clumsy or awkward never entered her mind. She matched him as perfectly as if their loving had been choreographed by the stars. With his every stroke she soared higher, until there was nothing but brilliant light and the earth-shattering climax that shook her body and drew his release deep within her body.

TEN

Dayna looked at the grocery cart piled high with food and shook her head. "Do you honestly think we'll be able to eat all that in a week?" Maybe if a gang of hungry mountain men came streaming into Aces High there would be a chance of polishing off everything Luke and the boys had heaped into the cart.

Then again, Luke might have taken into consideration her ravenous appetite that morning and doubled up on everything. For some strange reason, she had awakened in her bed tired, satisfied, and extremely hungry. The pancakes and eggs she had had for breakfast had done little to appease her newly developed appetite. She met Luke's gaze over the cart and flushed. The reason wasn't so strange, after all.

Luke had broken down every barrier she had ever erected. His kisses had not only promised heaven, they had taken her there. His touch had made her need, made her want, and he had satisfied those needs. Never had she experienced such emotion. Such wonder. But it had been Luke's responses to her touch that had given her the most happiness. He had not wanted her just to assuage some hunger or curiosity. He had taken her twice. Never before had she been made love to twice in one night. Steven had been wrong. She could experience and give passion—with the right man. It looked like Luke was the right man.

"We have to keep up our strength," Luke said in answer to her comment. His gaze caressed her face like a lover's touch.

"Oh." She glanced at Todd and Jesse who were hanging on their every word. "What do we have to keep our strength up for?" She trusted Luke not to make any unseemly remarks and wondered how he was going to get out of this one.

"Why, hiking of course." He grinned. "There's this really neat place the boys would just love."

"Where, Uncle Luke?" Jesse asked, practically jumping up and down with excitement.

"Yeah, where?" Todd asked.

"Which mountain do we have to climb?" Dayna mumbled, sighing. She knew when she was beaten. Three against one didn't seem fair to her, but she would follow her men anywhere. She glanced at all three males and smiled. Anyone looking at them now would think they were a normal family on their summer vacation.

Luke handed her the groceries as she placed them on the conveyer belt. "It's only a little mountain, Dayna." He winked at the teenage cashier who had been listening to their conversation.

"Don't believe him, ma'am." The teenager blew a huge pink bubble, allowed it to pop, then sucked the gum back into her mouth. "There's no such thing as a little mountain in Colorado."

Dayna laughed with the flame-haired girl, who was wearing four silver studs and a miniature skull in one ear. "Tell me about it. He already made me hike up two of them."

The girl gave Luke a hard stare out of black-rimmed eyes. "Shame on you."

"Hey." Luke raised his hands innocently into the air. "It was her idea to go camping."

"We're prospecting for gold," Jesse added importantly.

The girl grinned. "Any luck?"

"Naw," Todd said. "But we did meet this old prospector named Pete."

The smile faded from the cashier's mouth, and her hand froze in the act of passing a box of granola bars over the scanner. "Did you say an old prospector named Pete? One-eyed Pete?"

"That's the one."

"Do you know anything about him?" Dayna asked. She didn't like the way the color had drained from the girl's face. She had been pale enough to begin with.

The girl shook her head. "Only know what I

heard. Never seen him for myself." She went back to scanning the groceries.

"What have you heard?" Luke asked as he handed Dayna the last item from their cart.

"Heard he's usually found around an old abandoned town called Prosperity."

"Prosperity's name was changed nearly seventy years ago to Aces High," Luke said.

"We own it," Todd said proudly as he pointed to his younger brother. "Our grandpa Max left it to us when he died. It's a ghost town."

"But it doesn't have any ghosts," Jesse said with a sigh of disappointment.

The girl gave the boys a strange smile. "That was real nice of your grandfather." She weighed the bananas on a scale on top of the register. "He must have loved you very much to leave you a whole town."

"What else did you hear?" Dayna still had a hundred unanswered questions about Pete.

"Nothing much." The girl shrugged, but didn't meet Dayna's gaze. "People usually spot him around summertime and incredible luck usually happens to those he meets."

"Really?" Todd asked. "Do they strike it rich?"

"About ten years ago one guy won the lottery with a ticket he had purchased the day after he met Pete."

"No one found any gold?" Jesse asked. "We're looking for gold."

The girl shook her head. "Not that I know of,

sorry." She ran the last item over the scanner and totaled the groceries. "Weather's looking a lot better today than yesterday."

Luke handed the girl a stack of bills as Dayna placed the last bag into the cart. She knew a change of subject when she heard one, and the cashier obviously wanted to drop the subject of One-eyed Pete and his cantankerous mule Freckles. She dug into her purse and handed each of the boys a quarter, then nodded to the row of bubble gum machines by the exit. Neither boy needed further encouragement.

"How long have the stories of Pete been circulating?" she asked.

The girl carefully counted out Luke's change as she placed it into his hand along with the receipt. "I've heard the stories all my life."

That wasn't much help. The girl looked sixteen or seventeen. "Anything else we should know?"

"He's harmless, if that's what's bothering you."

"We already figured that out for ourselves. Any ideas on who he is or where he came from?"

"No one knows his last name or where he lives. There's a rumor that he's the grandson of an old prospector named Pete and some saloon gal named Annie who lived in Prosperity, I mean Aces High, when it was a real town."

Dayna smiled as Luke reached for her hand and gave it a gentle squeeze. Luke nodded at the girl. "That would explain how he knew so much about the town and its residents."

"I'm sure it would." The girl glanced at the customer waiting behind Luke and Dayna.

They took the hint and pushed their cart toward the exit where her sons waited. Dayna had her answer. It was so simple, she wondered why she hadn't thought of it before. The Pete they had met had been related to the old prospector Max had won the town from.

This new Pete was probably finding his roots and really enjoyed getting into the role. Why anyone would want to pull a mule through the Rockies was beyond her, but hey, in this day and age, anything was possible. That explanation beat the theory of Pete being a ghost. And the prospect of having something good happen to them was enticing. She glanced over at Luke and grinned. Something good had indeed happened to them since they met Pete. She had fallen in love.

Dayna awoke to the smell of fresh brewed coffee and bacon frying over the camp stove. She buried her face deeper into her pillow and smiled. She was in love! Glorious mind-blowing, body-shattering love! And it didn't matter one iota that Luke had been her brother-in-law. He was so different from Steven, she was beginning to have her doubts that they were brothers. Maybe Eileen and Joseph Callahan had adopted one or both of the boys. If she had to take a guess, she would say Luke was the adopted Callahan.

She raised her head and savored the aroma of breakfast being cooked for her. Not since she had left the safety and the security of her parents' home had someone actually cooked her breakfast without being paid to do so. Luke was an angel! She wiggled her toes in the warmth of her sleeping bag and giggled at the thought of Luke really being an angel. After what they'd done last night and the night before in his tent, while the boys slept so peacefully in hers, his wings would surely be clipped.

The man was insatiable. She was insatiable. He was truly a gifted lover. If she had to be truthful about it, she wasn't so bad herself. Luke seemed to honestly enjoy, encourage, and plead for her every touch. She was never clumsy or awkward. Everything just came so naturally to her when she was with him. Making love with Luke was perfect. Luke was perfect.

Dayna rolled over in her sleeping bag and squinted at the bright light flooding in through the nylon tent. She could hear the sounds of Todd and Jesse helping Luke and smiled. Luke was the perfect uncle, too, and he would make a wonderful father. Her smile faded. She shouldn't let her thoughts wander in that direction. She had no right placing Luke in a parental role for her sons.

He had told her a hundred times at least that he loved her, but had never once hinted at a future. He had shown her in countless ways how much he desired her. He genuinely seemed to like the boys and never crossed the boundary of propriety in front of them. They never even so much as held hands in front of the boys. Of course, there had been many stolen kisses when Jesse and Todd weren't looking. But there the relationship ended. No mention of the future, beyond what they would do the next day. Luke appeared to be holding something back. What, she didn't know, and she was afraid to ask. She had no right to ask.

She hadn't told him how she felt about him. She couldn't bring herself to tell him of her love. It was all so new, so different from what she had felt for Steven when she was twenty-two. She wasn't even sure she wanted to be in love with Luke, or any other man. Her life was finally on an even keel and she was enjoying her freedom. Her time was consumed by her job and her sons. Where would she find time for a man? Years before she had dreamed about what her future would be like. Now she was just satisfied with today.

So even if Luke wanted something more with her than just these few days, she wasn't sure if she'd be willing. No one knew better than she how big, how radical, a step marriage was. She might love Luke, but she'd need more than that before she'd be willing to make any sort of commitment to him. Yes, for now she'd just be satisfied with today.

"Hey, sleepyhead!" Luke yelled. "Rise and shine."

She laughed at the ridiculous situation two mature adults had found themselves in. In the middle of the night she had to crawl out of Luke's sleeping bag and into hers. Of all the romantic fantasies regarding the "morning after," being hollered at through a tent wasn't one of them. "I might rise," she called back, "but I refuse to shine."

Luke's and the boys' laughter filled the air. "Come on, Mom, we made the coffee," Todd said.

"Really?" Wasn't that sweet of her sons.

"Yeah. Uncle Luke says it's just the way you like it."

"How's that?" As far as she knew she only liked her coffee one way, hot.

"Strong enough to put hair on your chest," Todd yelled.

She bit her lip to hold back her laughter as she heard Luke choke and sputter on something. Obviously his coffee was going down the wrong pipe. "Oh, goodie, I can't wait to try it." She unzipped her sleeping bag. "Give me a minute to change and I'll be right out."

Five minutes later she was dressed, had made a call to nature, splashed a handful of frigid water onto her face, and brushed her teeth. She felt human, though not alluring or seductive. Anyone who found her desirable when she was dressed in old shorts and a T-shirt, with no makeup, and her hair perpetually pulled into a ponytail that fit through the back opening of her Colorado Rockies baseball cap, was either blind or her kind of man. Luke wasn't blind, so that left him being the man for her. At least for now.

She walked over to the tailgate of her Blazer, where Luke was manning the stove. "Where's the coffee I've been hearing about?" She wanted to greet him with a kiss, but the boys were watching.

"I don't know if I want you to drink it," he whispered. He glanced meaningfully at her chest.

She reached for the pot and poured herself a cup. "Nonsense. You're not the type to get jealous if my chest should sprout more hair than yours."

He glanced over his shoulder to make sure Todd and Jesse weren't within earshot. "I happen to love your chest just the way it is."

She brought the cup up to her mouth and gazed at him seriously over the rim. "Really? They aren't too small? Too saggy? If you look closely you can still see some faint stretch marks from when—"

"Stop it, Dayna." Luke glared at the pan of frying bacon as if he wanted to throw it. A muscle in his jaw ticked ominously. His lips barely moved as he grated out, "I'm not Steven."

"I didn't say you were!" She never thought he was Steven, or anything like him. But Luke was a man, and didn't men like perfect female bodies? After two kids her breasts would never be perky again. No matter how many sit-ups she did, her stomach would never be as flat as it was when she was twenty. Her legs had never gone on for miles, and gravity was influencing the direction her caboose was heading. She was a thirty-one-year-old mother of two. Her body would never be perfect in Luke's or any other man's eyes.

Luke was staring hard at her, and she could see there was a lot going on in his head. But he didn't respond. Todd's and Jesse's appearance near the Blazer probably had a lot to do with his silence.

"Is breakfast ready yet?" Todd asked. He peeked around Luke's back and hungrily eyed the crispy bacon.

Luke handed her the fork he'd been using to turn the bacon. "Your mother can dish out the bacon while I go get the eggs from the cooler."

She watched as he walked away, heading for the creek, where he had weighted down a Styrofoam cooler. The system he had devised so they could keep perishable items cold was part genius, part simplicity. Why hadn't she thought of weighing down a cooler, cutting a few holes into its side so the icy creek water flowed through, and storing such things as milk and eggs inside?

They might be getting bacon and eggs for breakfast this morning, but the jovial mood she had awakened to was gone. Luke obviously had some unresolved issues concerning Steven to deal with. When she'd first thought about Luke and her in a "romantic situation," she hadn't been able to separate the third-party ghost, namely Steven, who permeated the air around them. But once they'd made love, the ghost of Steven had vanished.

Maybe his ghost hadn't vanished for Luke. Maybe that was what was bothering him. Maybe it was Luke who couldn't separate *her* from his brother.

❖━━━❖

Luke squinted up into the early-afternoon sun and absently rubbed at his throbbing temples. He had to tell Dayna that he had been the reason behind Steven's cruel and unwarranted abusiveness. That morning when she'd joined him at the tailgate of her Blazer, he had wanted nothing more than to haul her into his arms and properly wish her a good morning. Todd and Jesse's presence had prevented the kiss, but not the desire.

Ever since the night in the motel, when she had come to him, he had wanted to shout to the world that they were lovers. That Dayna was finally his! But he had sensed she needed time to adjust, not only for herself, but for her sons. Uncle Luke showing up on a camping trip was one thing. Uncle Luke showing up in Mommy's bed was another.

The boys needed time to get used to the idea of him joining their family. Just like any other stepfather situation, it had to be approached with caution. It wasn't something you sprang on children overnight. But in their case it was a little more complicated. He was their uncle, who wanted to become their dad. Afternoon talk shows would have a ball with that topic. *Uncles who become Dads, and the nephews who become sons.*

There were two major problems with his plan for the future. First, he hadn't told Dayna he wanted to marry her and become the boys' stepfather. He had professed his love to her. There was no way he could hold that in any longer. Dayna needed to know exactly where he stood on that score. But the talk about their future he had been rehearsing was being played by ear. Dayna didn't seem ready to hear about the possibilities of marrying another Callahan. He couldn't blame her.

The many times he had spoken the words "I love you," they had never been reciprocated. He knew Dayna had feelings for him. He could see it in her eyes. Feel it in her touch. But it would do wonders if she would only speak the words. He needed to hear them. Her words would tell him this all hadn't been a dream and there was a chance for the future.

The second flaw in his master plan to win Dayna and her sons was that the boys hadn't been allowed to see him as anything other than an uncle. How were they ever going to adjust to him becoming their dad if they hadn't a clue he wanted to be their dad?

He needed to talk to Dayna. Honestly and openly. He needed to lay his cards on the table and accept whatever happened. If Max could win a ghost town with a pair of fives, surely he could win Dayna with the truth. The uncertainty and doubt that had been in her eyes that morning had plunged into his heart, nearly inflicting a lethal blow. Some part of Dayna still believed all those hateful and heartless words Steven must have spoken.

It had infuriated him that she apparently had been waiting for him to sink to his brother's level and criticize her. The temptation to throw the frying pan full of bacon toward the heavens had been great. Even beyond the grave Steven was winning. But

Steven had made a fatal mistake in his vindictiveness. He had underestimated the love Luke felt for Dayna. Never before had he fought for anything Steven had taken or destroyed. He had always stood by and watched his dreams crumble. But nothing had ever been as important as Dayna's love. He wasn't giving up. He would never give up.

Luke could hear the boyish laughter of Todd and Jesse as they splashed each other in the creek. The boys were having the time of their lives and were safely occupied. He wouldn't get another chance to talk to Dayna until the boys were asleep that night. What he wanted to say couldn't wait any longer.

He headed in the direction of the boys' laughter, spotted them in the creek just as he had pictured them, and waved. Dayna wasn't around. She must be back at camp. He headed in that direction. The boys would be safe enough. The creek was barely eleven inches deep in the spot where they were playing, and the chance of any wild animals coming within a mile of them was nonexistent. Both of the boys were making such a loud racket, even the birds were staying away.

Luke spotted Dayna dumping an armful of wood for their nightly fire onto the ground. He should have brought some back with him, but his mind had been preoccupied with other matters. Dayna, to be precise. He walked up behind her, wrapped his arms around her waist, and pressed a kiss to the back of her neck. She smelled of wild berry shampoo with a hint of bacon. She smelled good enough to eat. His mouth caressed the sensitive spot behind her ear. "Hi."

She leaned against him. "Hi, yourself." She arched her neck to give him better access. "Where are the boys?"

"Down at the creek experimenting on a new panning technique."

"Really?"

"Yeah." His mouth skimmed lower. "It's a process they developed all on their own. They kick all the water from the creek, so only the gold nuggets remain. That way they can walk along the empty creekbed and pluck the suckers right up."

Dayna chuckled. "Sounds like something they would do." She turned in his arms and raised her mouth toward his. "Kiss me quick."

"I'll kiss you any way I can." He captured her mouth and did her bidding. When the rising heat threatened to engulf them both, he broke the kiss and placed a couple of inches between them. He tenderly cupped her cheek. "We need to talk."

She glanced in the direction of the creek; the boy's laughter could still be heard. "About?"

"The past."

He watched as the excitement and desire she had been feeling the moment before faded from her face. She sighed heavily and said, "I'm sick to death of talking about the past, Luke. What was said, done, or thought in the past is over with. Can't we just forget it?"

He took her hand and pulled her toward the

folding chairs sitting near the rock circle for their fires. "This is too important to forget, Dayna. Sit, please."

She gave him a strange look, but sat.

He moved his chair so he was facing her, and leaned forward to capture her hands. "I'm not sure where to begin." He squeezed her fingers, assembled his thoughts, and sighed. "Steven had this sibling rivalry thing with me. He wanted what I had or what I wanted. If he couldn't get it, he destroyed it. I think his theory was, 'If I can't have it, neither can Luke.' "

"I figured that out years ago, Luke. Steven was highly sensitive to anything you did or accomplished. It got so it was just better for everyone if your name wasn't mentioned too often." She gave him a sad smile. "Sorry."

"Don't be sorry, love. You had nothing to do with Steven's problems. They started years before he met you. When we were little, he stole or broke just about every toy I owned. As we grew older he learned to hide his destructive ways better, but the end result was the same. He also learned to read people better. As you yourself admitted, Steven had a knack for finding a person's weak spot and using it against them. Steven knew instinctively what caught my eye, and he ruined it before I could even touch it."

"Is that why you moved so far away?"

"Partly." He glanced down at their clasped hands. "I also wanted to make it on my own without using the Callahan name. There were too many doors in Denver that could be opened with that name. I wanted to go someplace where the doors only opened if I made them open."

"I'm afraid Steven has permanently closed most of those doors, Luke. He used the Callahan name without thought or conscience. During his short life he ruined much that Max and your father accomplished."

"Max did it all, Dayna. My father rode on his father's coattails. He just had a lucky star when it came to business. Joseph Callahan was a lousy father and a lousier husband."

"I know."

"Like father, like son." He wasn't going to sugarcoat it to Dayna. She knew too much of the Callahan history.

"Like father, like *one* son."

His gaze locked with hers. He knew exactly what she was saying. She had separated him from his brother. His fingers trembled as they squeezed hers. "Thank you." Now for the hard part. "As I said, Steven tried to destroy anything I wanted." He took a deep breath. "Steven knew I wanted you."

She flushed wildly, but held his gaze. "He didn't destroy me, Luke. I'm successful at my chosen career. I can support myself and my sons. But my most important accomplishments are my sons. Todd and Jesse are my pride, my joy, and my love. Steven wasn't the perfect husband or father, but he gave me something very dear to me. To destroy me he would have had to go through his sons."

"That only proves my point, Dayna. Don't you see? He didn't want to destroy you, he wanted to ruin you for any other man." He saw the confusion in her eyes. "He wanted to fill your head with so much self-doubt and humiliation that you would never willingly give yourself to another man." His heart ached as huge tears filled her eyes. "He wanted to make sure you would never give yourself to me."

She shook her head and blinked rapidly. "That's not true."

"Think back, Dayna. When did he start tormenting you? I can't believe it was at the beginning of your marriage. You're not the kind to stay with a man you don't love, unless you had your sons to consider. You stayed with Steven because of the boys, didn't you?"

She nodded, silent.

"Did the harassment start right after Jesse was born?"

Her eyes widened. "How did you . . ."

"I flew in for Jesse's christening, remember? After the church service we all went back to your place. That's when Steven asked to borrow more money."

"More money?"

"I'd already loaned him quite a bit. He blew it on some sham investment. I refused to lend him any more. I told him to be a man for once in his life and get a job to support his family since he couldn't make his trust payments stretch from quarter to quarter."

Dayna closed her eyes as if in pain. "What did he say to that?"

"I won't repeat his exact words, but the gist of it was that I wanted him to fail so that you would leave him and then you'd be free for me." He could see the understanding dawning across her face. "He tormented you to get back at me, Dayna."

"Back at you?"

"Steven must have known he was losing you." He stroked her ashen cheek. "He found your vulnerable spot, love, and went in for the kill. You're a wonderful woman, Dayna, and I love you. But you must overcome the past so we can start to build a future together."

She stood up and looked wildly around. "What future? You've never mentioned anything about a future."

He stood. The violent trembling of her body alarmed him. She looked pale and ready to bolt. "Of course we're going to have a future, Dayna."

"There's no 'of course' about it, Luke." She flung her arm in the direction of his tent, where they had made love for the past two nights. "Just because we made love doesn't mean we're going to live happily ever after."

"We're getting married, Dayna. Make no mistake about it." He ran a hand down his face and wished he could call back his blunt words. This wasn't exactly how he'd planned on asking Dayna to marry him.

She took a step back. "Don't tell me what I am or am not going to do, Luke. I took all of that that I could take from your brother. I'm not going to take it from you or any other man."

Steven, Steven, Steven. He was sick to death of Steven. "Let's leave Steven out of this, Dayna. From now on it's between you and me."

She swiped at the tears rolling down her face. "I thought we were at least friends. Obviously I was wrong."

"Friends! I don't want to be your friend, Dayna." He wanted to be her husband. He reached out to grab her shoulders, but she again moved back.

"Fine! We aren't friends. We aren't lovers. We're nothing. Whatever we had is over, Luke. I would appreciate it if you would just—"

"Mom!" Todd yelled as he raced across the dirt toward the arguing adults. "Mom!"

Dayna swiped the tears from her face before turning toward her son.

Luke frowned as he watched Todd race toward them. Something was wrong. Terribly wrong. He started running toward the boy half a second after Dayna. His gaze shot from Todd's white face to the empty land behind him. Where was Todd's shadow? Where was Jesse?

"Mom!" Todd cried one last time as both adults reached him. He threw himself into his mother's arms. "Jesse's gone!"

ELEVEN

Dayna cupped her hands around her mouth and yelled, "Jesse!" Her voice was beginning to crack and fade, but not her resolve. They would find Jesse. They had to find Jesse. No answering yell reached her ears, though. For the past forty-five minutes she and Todd had been searching near the camp, in case he should find his way back. Luke had set off in the direction Todd had last seen Jesse. He had enough equipment strapped to his back to survive for a week in the mountains.

She didn't understand why Luke had insisted on taking ropes, blankets, and a first-aid kit just to find one small boy. Jesse couldn't have wandered too far. He'd been missing for less than an hour. She refused to think about all the danger he could find himself in that would require Luke to open that backpack. All she wanted was Jesse back safe and sound.

Why had he wandered away from his brother?

And why hadn't he obeyed the simple rule she had drummed into both of the boys' heads since their first camping trip? *If you ever find yourself lost, stop, stand right where you are, and listen for someone calling your name.* It was such a simple rule, surely a six-year-old could comprehend and follow it. So why hadn't Jesse?

Fear gripped her heart again, but she smiled reassuringly at Todd. "Don't worry. Uncle Luke has probably found him by now." Todd looked terrible. His nose and eyes were red and swollen from crying. He didn't believe her. She bent down and gave him a hug. "It will be okay, honey. We'll find him."

"I'm sorry, Mom." Todd pressed his tearstained face against her shoulder and shuddered. "I should have been watching him better."

"No, honey." She grabbed his shoulders and forced him to look at her. "It's *not* your fault. I'm the one who should have been paying closer attention to you two. I'm the mother, Todd. It's my fault. I never should have left you two alone."

"We only wanted to get some wood for tonight's fire." Todd swiped the back of his hand across his eyes. A streak of dirt was left behind. "I told him to pick up the little sticks, but he said he wanted to find a big log so Luke would be proud of him."

So Luke would be proud of him. Jesse had been trying to please Luke, not her. It showed her how much the boys had come to love their uncle. She couldn't fault them for that. She had fallen in love with him too. And now he was mapping out their future without talking to her about it. Telling her they were getting married, not asking.

She shook her head, forcing all thoughts of Luke out of her mind. She had more important things to think about, like her sons. The one who was lost and the one who blamed himself. "That was very thoughtful of you to want to gather wood, Todd, but you should have told me you were leaving the creek so I could come with you." She pulled him back into her arms and squeezed. "Next time we gather the wood together, okay?"

"Okay."

Both of them jumped as the sound of a loud piercing whistle reached their ears. It was Luke's signal. Jesse had been found! Dayna brushed at the tears of joy filling her eyes and hugged Todd closer. "See, I told you Luke would find him." She stood up and grabbed Todd's hand. "Come on, slowpoke, let's go see your brother." Her silent prayers had been answered.

She pulled Todd up the mountain in the direction of Luke's whistle. Luke had found her son! She'd known he would. She had never seen a man snap into action before, but that was exactly what he had done the minute they had gotten the story from Todd. Luke had quickly, but calmly, assembled a pack. Then he had hauled her into his arms, told her their discussion wasn't over, and that he'd find Jesse. Then he'd done something shocking. He had kissed her right in front of a wide-eyed Todd. She had just stood there speechless. What in the world had Luke been thinking to kiss her like that in front of Todd? Hadn't she, not five minutes before that, told him to leave?

She tripped over an exposed root in her hurry to reach her son while thinking about Luke's kisses and ended up kissing the ground. Todd chuckled and helped her get up. "Come on, Mom. Now who's the slowpoke?"

"I guess I am." She looked around. They should be near the spot where Luke had whistled, but she didn't see any signs of him or Jesse. She hoped they weren't heading down the mountain while she and Todd were heading up. She looked at Todd. "Keep very quiet and listen."

She cupped her mouth and hollered, "Jesse!" She waited a heartbeat, then yelled, "Luke!"

An answering call was farther up the mountain and to the left. She grinned at Todd and they both took off in that direction. Five minutes later they stumbled out of a particularly thick batch of trees onto rocky ground. She spotted Luke working with a coil of rope, but no Jesse. She glanced frantically around and ran toward Luke.

He dropped the rope he had been tying, stood up, and caught her in his arms.

"Where's Jesse?"

"Don't panic, Dayna. I need you calm and I need you now. We don't have a lot of time."

"Oh my God!" She looked around again and could only spot Todd who had joined them. Her gaze shot to the ravine a good forty feet to their left.

With terror-filled insight, she knew the answer before she asked the question. "Where is he?"

Luke stepped into the harness he'd designed from the coil of rope and tightened it around his waist. He gave Todd a reassuring smile. "Your brother is going to be all right, but I need your mother's and your help, okay?"

"Okay."

"Luke?"

"Todd, you go stand over there." He pointed to a tree. "I don't want you near the edge." He took hold of Dayna's hand and led her toward the ravine. "Whatever you do, don't call to him."

Her voice was barely a squeak as it left her mouth. "Why?"

"You'll see." He knelt down near the edge and motioned for her to do the same. "Lie down flat and try not to send any rocks over the edge." He slowly made his way to the edge with Dayna beside him.

Dayna didn't want to look over the edge, but knew she had to. Her son was down there. As she'd approached the ravine she hadn't seen anything but a deep rocky gorge cut into the mountain. She hadn't seen a bottom. Luke had promised Todd that Jesse was going to be all right, and Luke didn't lie.

She forced herself to peer over the side and felt her heart threaten to leave her throat. Jesse was right below her, only ten or twelve feet away. Ten or twelve impossible feet. He was lying on a very narrow ledge and he wasn't moving. She had to ask, had to know. "Is he . . ."

"He's breathing, Dayna, but it looks like his right arm is broken." Luke started to slide back, motioning her to follow. "He's either unconscious from the fall, or he passed out from the pain."

Dayna didn't move. She didn't want to leave her son.

"Come on, Dayna. We have to work fast, before he comes to." Luke grabbed the back of her jeans and hauled her away from the edge. "If he rolls off the ledge . . ."

She didn't need him to finish the sentence. She knew what would happen if Jesse fell. It was a straight drop of over thirty feet onto jagged rocks. Jesse wouldn't survive. She quickly came to her feet. They had to get help, and get it fast. "What do we do?" She remembered seeing a phone booth at the service station about fourteen miles from Aces High. If she or Luke hurried they could have help within an hour.

"I need you and Todd to help pull Jesse up, once I have him secured."

"Pull him up?" She glanced between the ravine and the rope harness tied around Luke's waist. Her stomach tightened into one large knot and dropped to her knees. "You're going down there!"

"Someone has to, and it's got to be done now. There's no time to call for help, Dayna." He caressed her cheek. "I promise to take really good care of him, love."

She tasted blood as she bit her lower lip. Luke was risking his life to save her son. She watched helplessly as he checked the ropes one last time and said a few comforting words to Todd. Luke's concern and love for her boys overwhelmed her.

Luke handed her one end of another coiled rope. "When I yell, I need you to lower this rope. I'll be tying it around Jesse. Hopefully I'll be able to bring him to, but don't count on it. Then I'll give you the signal to start hauling him up. It's only about eleven feet, so it won't be that bad. Don't worry if the rope slips, he won't fall." He nodded to a distant tree where the other end of the rope was tied. "The rope's tied, plus I'll be guiding him up the best I can."

Her fingers trembled around the length of orange nylon rope. "The ledge isn't wide enough to hold you both."

"You let me worry about the ledge." He brushed her mouth with a soft kiss. "You just haul when I say haul." He walked toward the edge and positioned himself.

"Luke!" He glanced up. "Please be careful." His smile tugged at her heart. "I . . . I . . ." For some reason the words of love she wanted to say lodged in her throat. She swallowed hard and said, "Thank you."

He nodded, then slowly disappeared over the side.

Dayna hurried to the edge, and once again very carefully peered over the side. Jesse hadn't moved. She held her breath as Luke descended the eleven feet, then cautiously made his way over to where

Jesse lay. The ledge wasn't wide enough to hold him, so he tied off his rope and hung suspended at Jesse's level. It seemed like hours, when in fact it was only minutes, before she saw Jesse stir. She wanted to yell out, but was terrified she would startle her son and he would fall off the ledge. Luke blocked most of her view as he examined the boy.

Finally, Luke looked up and gave her a reassuring smile. "His arm is broken, and he has a bump on the back of his head, but besides that he appears okay. He seems coherent and is willing to help us get him up and out of here."

Dayna could hear Jesse quietly weeping. Each sob tore at her heart. She wanted to trade places with him. She wanted him out of the ravine and in her arms. "Jesse, honey, you listen to Uncle Luke. I know your arm must hurt real bad. I promise, as soon as you're up here we'll get you to a doctor who will make it all better." She could see the funny angle in which his little arm lay across his stomach. But at least there wasn't any blood. If there had been blood she didn't think she could hold it together.

Jesse moaned and nodded.

Luke took a hunk of fabric that had been hanging from the back pocket of his jeans and started to rip it into strips using his teeth. Dayna recognized it as one of his T-shirts and silently promised herself she'd buy Luke a drawer full of shirts to replace it. With great caution, care, and love, Luke secured Jesse's broken arm to his chest, so it wouldn't move too much. Dayna counted three cries of pain from her son; each one pierced her heart.

When the last of the strips was tied, Luke glanced up. "Lower the rope, Dayna."

She lowered the rope and held her breath as Luke maneuvered Jesse into a sitting position, then expertly tied the rope around his waist. When the rope was secured, Luke helped Jesse to stand, facing the rock wall.

"Okay, Dayna, start pulling, but do it slowly."

Dayna hurried from the ravine and gave Todd the thumbs-up sign. "Ready, Todd?"

Todd gripped the rope with both hands and nodded.

Dayna knew that Todd's strength wasn't going to add a lot toward hauling Jesse up. His participation in rescuing his brother was more for his benefit than Jesse's. She knew that was why Luke had included Todd in the rescue operation. She grabbed hold of the rope and pulled with all her might. Jesse's fifty-five pounds felt like a hundred and fifty-five.

Within five minutes, Jesse and Luke were both safely out of the ravine. As Luke and Todd packed up the ropes, Dayna held Jesse in her arms. Both of them were crying.

Five hours later Luke silently entered Jesse's hospital room. The boy appeared to be sleeping comfortably, and Dayna was right beside him holding his little scraped hand. She was one amazing woman. One amazing mother. She hadn't let go of Jesse since Luke had carried him down the mountain and placed him in the backseat of her Blazer, then driven them all to the nearest hospital in Boulder. It had taken him and two nurses to talk her into releasing Jesse long enough for the X rays to be taken of his head and arm. Jesse had a possible concussion, a hairline fracture of the skull, and a broken ulna bone. They were going to keep him overnight and if all was well, release him in the morning.

Luke softly closed the door behind him, and Dayna looked up. "I've brought you a change of clothes." He walked to the bed and handed her a brown paper bag.

"Where's Todd?"

"Down at the nurses' station being fussed over. It must be a slow night around here because they just offered him a drink and some cookies."

"Are you sure he's all right?"

"He's fine." He nodded at the sleeping Jesse. "How's the patient?"

"Resting comfortably. They gave him a shot to help ease the pain. They didn't want to give him anything that would put him to sleep because of the head injury." She reluctantly released her son's hand. "Did you find a hotel?"

"Todd and I got a room at one right down the street." He reached into his shirt pocket and pulled out a slip of paper. "Here's the number in case you need us." He glanced around the room. "Why don't you go on down to the cafeteria and grab yourself something to eat. I'll stay with Jesse."

"I already ate. A nurse brought me in a tray about forty minutes ago." She opened the bag and glanced inside. "Can you stay with Jesse while I go get cleaned up and changed?"

What did she expect him to do, he wondered, turn around and leave Jesse all alone in some strange hospital room? Lord, her opinion of him must rate somewhere just above a cockroach. "Take your time, Dayna." With a weary sigh he lowered himself into the chair she had just vacated. "I'm in no hurry."

She grabbed her purse and the bag and disappeared into Jesse's bathroom. Ten minutes later, a remarkably better looking Dayna reemerged. Her dirty top and torn shorts had been replaced by a clean T-shirt and a pair of comfortable sweatpants. Thick white socks cushioned her feet. Her hair was neatly brushed, and her face was scrubbed clean. All traces of her earlier tears were gone. She looked sweet and clean and entirely kissable. She looked beautiful.

Luke turned away from that thought and Dayna and concentrated on getting Jesse back home. "Weather for tomorrow looks good. We should have a quick and easy drive to Denver."

"We?" She placed the bag of dirty clothes and her purse on top of the built-in dresser and walked over to the window.

"You don't think I would allow you to drive all

the way to Denver alone with just Todd to help with Jesse, do you?"

"What about your Jeep?" A frown pulled at her brows. "I still have the tent and a bunch of other stuff back at Aces High."

"Don't worry, that's all been taken care of." He stood and joined her at the window. Night was slowly falling on the city. "The rental car will be returned and all your camping and panning equipment will be delivered to your house the day after tomorrow."

"How did you manage that?"

"All it takes is a phone call." With a phone and a credit card, a man could move a mountain. Luke turned away from the window and stared down at the sleeping boy. Jesse and Todd had become very important to him during the past week. More important than just a pair of adorable and loving nephews. He loved them as if they were his own sons. "You have more important things to think about than a tent and a bunch of sieves."

"The doctor assured me, just before you arrived, that Jesse will be all right."

"And he will." Luke smiled and slowly reached out, touching Jesse's foot. Jesse wasn't the first, nor would he be the last, little boy to wander away and find himself in serious trouble. Luke just thanked whatever lucky star had been shining down on him that had allowed him to spot a track or two of Jesse's and to see where the ground had recently broken away at the edge of that ravine. Curiosity and a sense of dread had made him peer over the edge. He was just damn thankful that Jesse was all right. "When I said you had more important things to think about, Dayna, I was referring to us."

"Us?"

"Our conversation wasn't over. I know you have a lot on your mind, but before Todd and I head back to the hotel for the night, we need to talk."

He turned away from the bed and faced her. "I love you, Dayna." Lifting a hand, he tenderly caressed her cheek. "I know I sprang it on you all of a sudden this afternoon, and my technique definitely could use improvement, but the question remains. Will you marry me?"

"Marriage?" Dayna shuddered and refused to raise her gaze above his chest. "Sometimes marriages have a way of not working out, Luke. It's not that easy."

He cupped her chin and forced her gaze upward. "Could be as simple as second time lucky."

"It's not just me, Luke. There's the boys to consider."

"I don't think it's the boys holding you back, Dayna." His thumb stroked her jaw. "You know how much the boys mean to me, and I don't think they would have a problem with me becoming their stepfather."

She glanced nervously at the bed. "I could never repay you for what you did for Jesse today, Luke."

"I'm not asking you to." He followed her gaze to

the sleeping boy. "I didn't do anything for Jesse that I wouldn't have done for any other boy."

She smiled. "In their eyes you're a hero."

"What am I in your eyes?" There, he had finally asked. Sooner or later she had to tell him what she felt. Was that love he saw in her eyes when she looked at him, or gratitude? He had shown Dayna, every way he knew how, how desirable and beautiful she was. He hadn't done it for her gratitude, he had done it for love.

Tears filled her eyes. "You're a hero, Luke. You saved Jesse's life."

"Dammit, Dayna. I don't want to be your or anyone else's hero." In frustration he ran his fingers through his hair. "Can't you see, that's not what I want from you?"

"What do you want, Luke?"

"I want to wake up beside you for the rest of my life. I want to grow old with you. I want to become the father Jesse and Todd never had. In short, Dayna, I want a future. I want to get married. I want 'happily ever after.' "

"What if I can no longer believe in 'happily ever after'?"

He gave her a slow, warm smile. "You believe."

"How do you know what I believe?"

"I've seen it when you look at your sons. When Jesse was missing, you didn't give up. Even when he lay broken and unconscious on a ledge a mere five inches from death, you never gave up. You knew it was all going to work out. You wouldn't have settled for anything less." He reached out and caressed her swollen lower lip, which she had gnawed during the forty-minute drive to the hospital. "You believed, Dayna."

"Jesse is my son, Luke. I love him beyond life."

"As it should be." He held her gaze and waited. This was where she was supposed to confess her love and they would all find that "happily ever after." Dayna's silence stretched into an awkward moment. Sighing, he lowered his hand and turned away. "I see."

"What do you see, Luke?"

"I was deluding myself into thinking you could love me."

"Luke . . ."

"Don't say it, Dayna. The odds were insurmountable to begin with. Steven made sure the deck was stacked in his favor."

"Steven . . ." Her voice broke, tears blocking her throat. "Steven has nothing to do with how I feel about you."

"Steven might as well be standing physically between us, Dayna. He's there, larger than life. Make no mistake about it, Steven punished you because of me. If you could never forgive me for that, I'll have to accept it. But I didn't make love to you just to prove Steven was wrong or to right any injustice from the past. *We* made love because it was what *we* both wanted to do."

She reached out a hand to him, but let it fall

when he backed farther away. "I know," she whispered.

His gaze had followed her hand as she'd dropped it back to her side. If he had allowed her to touch him, he wouldn't have had the strength not to pull her into his arms and kiss her. She hadn't come right out and said she wouldn't marry him, or that she didn't love him. There was still a shadow of a chance for a future with her and the boys.

"Don't throw away our future for the wrong reason, Dayna. I love you, and I love Todd and Jesse as if they were my own. I want us to have a future together. I want us to be a family."

"A family?"

The sound of Todd opening the door stopped her next words. The way she had whispered the word *family* gave him hope. That one simple word had sounded like it held every one of her dreams, but he couldn't tell.

"Hey, Mom, is Jesse sleeping?"

"Shh. Yes he is, and let's keep him that way." She walked over to Todd and hugged him. "I want you to listen to Uncle Luke and behave tonight. Jesse should be ready to go home sometime before lunch tomorrow."

"Home?"

"Home." She ruffled Todd's hair. "Our camping trip seems to be cut short."

"Is Uncle Luke coming with us?"

"Sure am, buddy." He joined Todd by the door

but kept his gaze on Dayna. She refused to meet his eyes.

"Oh, then it's okay." Todd reached up and gave his mother a kiss on the cheek, then glanced once more at the bed. "Tell Jesse I'll see him in the morning."

"We'll be here waiting."

Luke hustled Todd out of the door before turning back toward Dayna. "Think about what I said, Dayna. I believe. Do you?" He glanced once more at the sleeping boy, then left the room.

TWELVE

Dayna stood by the window of Jesse's room and watched as the lights of Boulder slowly diminished, one by one. Jesse had awakened an hour ago, asking for a drink of water before falling asleep again. He didn't seem too uncomfortable, and his gentle even breathing filled her with peace. Her son was safe.

If only she could rest too. In the three hours since Luke and Todd had left, she had paced the shine off the sterile green and white tile floor. Jesse was going to be fine. All she had to worry about now was her future, or her lack of one.

Luke had been wrong. Steven wasn't standing between them any longer. Her late husband had ceased to matter the night she and Luke had first made love. Her fears of the future didn't include worrying about if she could please Luke physically. She already knew she could. No, her fears went much deeper than that. She didn't know if she was strong enough to again marry the man she loved, knowing it might all disintegrate. How would she survive if Luke decided he no longer wanted to be married to her?

From the day she'd walked down the aisle, a virgin staring starry-eyed at the future, to the night she had asked Steven to leave, it had taken seven years for their love to die. It had been a painful death. She had struggled to handle everything maturely and calmly, while inside she had screamed and cried. How could she subject herself to such pain again?

She had been strong for her sons. They deserved to have at least one parent who was stable and never faltered. What would happen to them if a second marriage failed? Todd and Jesse deserved a loving stepfather. Hell, they had deserved a loving father, but since that had never materialized, a stepfather would have to do. Luke loved the boys and they loved him in return. He would never purposely hurt them. But if they did marry, and the boys looked to him as a father, they would be hurt if the marriage fell apart, and she would be even more devastated knowing she had caused her sons that pain.

Luke was right, though. Despite her concern for her sons, they weren't preventing her from committing herself to him. It was her fear of failing. What if Luke stopped loving her? What if he was taken from her, as her parents had been? What if he hated being married? What if, what if, what if . . .

Dayna walked away from the window and sat down on her makeshift bed of two chairs. What if there was a "happily ever after" and she didn't reach for it? She wrapped the blanket one of the nurses had left for her around her shoulders and yawned. Lying down, she wiggled her bottom until she found the most comfortable position. What if her dreams were all within her grasp, but she didn't reach for them? She placed her head on the lumpy pillow and stared at her son.

The pale shaft of light coming in through the cracked door touched his face. He looked like an angel, all tousled golden hair and pink cheeks. His lips were slightly parted, and she could see each breath he took. She smiled and closed her eyes. Her family was safe.

A family!

Wasn't that what Luke wanted to be part of, a family? Why was she so afraid of something she wanted so much? *A family!* Even the sound of it made her want to believe in the future. A tiny frown marred her brow as sleep finally claimed her for the night.

Dayna anxiously paced the small hospital room. Where were Luke and Todd? They'd said they'd be there by ten, and it was now five minutes after. She had something very important to tell Luke and her sons.

Jesse tugged at the blanket on his bed. "I thought you said they were coming?"

"They are, honey." She crossed back over to the

bed and brushed back a lock of his hair. "They should be here any minute."

As if on cue Todd skidded into the room. "Hey, Jesse, how are you feeling?"

"Okay." He proudly showed Todd his cast. "Dr. Beamer signed my cast this morning when he came to check on me."

Todd peeked into the sling to get a better look. "Hey, cool. Can I sign my name?"

"Sure." Jesse looked at Luke, who had followed Todd into the room at a more leisurely pace. "Did you bring my clothes?"

"Sure did, kid." Luke held up a paper bag. "A nurse at the station just told me that as soon as you're dressed, you're free to leave."

Dayna took the bag from Luke without looking at him. "Let's go into the bathroom, young man, and get you ready."

Jesse didn't need any further prompting. Within five minutes he was neatly dressed and ready to leave. Todd had found the remote and was sitting on the bed watching cartoons.

Dayna smiled as Luke laughed at something Bugs Bunny did. Men were still little boys at heart. "Hey, Todd," she said, "would you keep an eye on Jesse for a minute? I need to talk with Luke."

Todd looked uncertain. Dayna knew he was still feeling guilty about yesterday, and he needed to know she trusted him. "It's okay, honey," she said. "We'll be right next door."

She eyed Jesse. "And you. Listen to your brother and no more wandering off on your own."

"Yes, Mom." Jesse climbed onto the bed and settled down next to Todd.

Todd smiled. Dayna nodded, then glanced at Luke. "May I have a word with you for a minute?" Without waiting for his answer, she walked out the door. The room next to Jesse's was empty. All she needed was a few minutes of privacy. Hopefully she could get it in there. She wasn't about to suffer through the drive back to Denver without having this conversation first.

Luke followed her into the room and stood back as she closed the door. He looked good enough to kiss this morning, all freshly shaven and clean. She, on the other hand, probably looked like something a cat wouldn't drag in. She was wearing the same clothes she'd slept in, if you could call lying on two chairs with a blanket sleeping. She didn't.

She moved farther into the room. "Last night you gave me a lot to think about."

"I know everything has been happening so fast, Dayna."

He seemed a little nervous, and she took that as a good sign. "I did a lot of thinking last night, Luke. I realized quite a lot of things about myself. First being, you made me realize that I'm not frigid, or unresponsive, or whatever people call it. I felt and did things with you that I've never felt or done before in my life. You showed me what being a woman is all about. For that I must thank you, but I won't marry you because of it."

"But—"

"You had your turn last night. Let me finish." She ran her fingers along the footboard of the empty bed. "You also made me realize how much you love my sons. You risked your life to save Jesse, something I assure you his own father never would have done." She shot Luke a quick glance to gauge his reaction. "But I won't marry you because you love my sons and they love you."

He didn't look happy about the way the conversation was heading, and she secretly smiled.

He took a step toward her, and she held up her hand to stop him. "There's only one reason that I'll be marrying you, Lucas Ryan Callahan."

He seemed to stop breathing for a moment, then he advanced on her and growled, "And that is?"

Her smile lit the room. "I love you, Luke Callahan, and I want that 'happily ever after.' "

She was in his arms and kissing him before she could complete her sentence. When he finally lifted his mouth she softly asked, "Become my family, Luke?"

"It's all I've ever dreamed about." His mouth teased the corner of her lip.

"You realize," she went on, "your mother is going to have a coronary, people will undoubtedly talk, and the boys will be ecstatic."

"Don't worry. Mother's heart will withstand the strain of our happiness. People will talk regardless of what we do." His mouth brushed hers. "And no one, not even the boys, could be happier than I am at this moment."

"Should we go break the news that their uncle is about to become their stepfather?"

His mouth skimmed her neck. "In a minute. I have something more important to do."

"Like what?"

"Like kiss my future bride."

Luke nuzzled the back of Dayna's neck. "Are they asleep?"

She tilted her head and gave him better access. "Both are sleeping like babies." The drive home from Boulder had been uneventful, yet long. Luke had insisted on stopping nearly a dozen times so the boys could stretch their legs and not become too cramped. Jesse had been cranky, but Luke had handled him like a pro. He was going to make a wonderful stepfather.

"Are you sure you want me to stay the night?" he asked. "I could grab a hotel room."

His lips were caressing her shoulder while his hands were stroking her flowing skirt. Her bed was just a short trip down the hall, and he had been driving her crazy all day with stolen kisses and playful winks. "Not on your life, Callahan." She leaned back into his hard body and did some stroking of her own. "I'll toss your butt out of my bed before daylight so the boys won't see you there. You can bunk on the couch."

She felt his smile against her collarbone. "We're not even married yet and already you're making me sleep on the couch."

"Well, don't get used to it." She gripped his jean-clad thighs. "I have plans for that gorgeous butt of yours."

Luke growled as she wiggled her bottom. "Promises, promises." He raised his head and glanced around her kitchen. "What else do you have to lock up?"

"Impatient?"

"For you? Definitely." He pulled her into his arms and kissed her until she couldn't breathe. Finally he raised his head. "How does Saturday sound for our wedding?"

"This Saturday?" It was Sunday evening. Was he out of his mind?

"No, Saturday three years from now." He captured the surprised *O* of her mouth with a kiss. "Of course this Saturday. You said you didn't want anything fancy. Just a few close friends. Todd and Jesse seem okay with the idea."

Todd and Jesse seemed more than okay with the idea of Luke becoming their stepfather. They were thrilled. They had talked of nothing else all day long. It was the other member of the family causing her concern. Eileen Callahan was going to have a stroke. Not only because Luke was marrying her, but because they'd agreed that his home outside of Washington was the logical place to live.

"What about your mother?"

"What about her?"

"We should at least tell her we're getting married, Luke. She is your mother and the boys' grandmother."

"Couldn't we just fax her a copy of the certificate after the fact?"

"No." She ran her hand through his thick hair, loving the feel of it. "When the boys and I called her this evening, she sounded strange."

"In what way?"

"Well, she sounded nice."

Luke chuckled. "That is strange."

She playfully punched him in the arm. "I'm not kidding, Luke. She sounded different, and she said she had something very important to discuss with us when we go visit her tomorrow morning."

"Oh, goodie, I can't wait."

Dayna wiggled her eyebrows and ran a finger down the buttons on his shirt. "Neither can I."

He grinned and captured her wayward finger before it danced below his belt buckle. "I'm marrying a tease!"

She started to unbutton his shirt. "Teases don't come through on what they promise, Luke." She placed a line of kisses down his chest. "I plan on delivering the goods."

He swung her up into his arms and headed down the hallway, nipping her earlobe. "I love your *goods.*"

"Shhh . . ." She giggled. "You'll wake the boys."

He stopped in the middle of the hall and stared at the boys' closed bedroom doors. "Is this what marriage is all about?"

Dayna chewed her lower lip for a second. "I'm afraid so, Luke. It's not too late to back out."

He grinned and shook his head. "You're not going to get rid of me that easy, Dayna. I like knowing the boys are there." He continued down the hall toward the master bedroom. "I also like knowing you're going to be waking up beside me every morning."

"Not tomorrow morning. You're going to be waking up on a couch that's probably six inches too short."

Luke softly closed the door behind them. "How do you feel about getting married on a Wednesday?"

Luke squeezed Dayna's hand as they walked toward his mother's sitting room. The boys had dashed in before them to show off Jesse's cast and to shout that they had great news that was a secret. They could hear Eileen's concerned "Oh my's" as she heard the story about how Jesse broke his arm. Luke and Dayna entered the room and stopped. Standing next to Eileen's chair was a man. He appeared to be around sixty, but the thing that surprised them both was his resemblance to Steven. If Steven had lived to be sixty, he would look exactly like the man who had a comforting hand on Eileen's shoulder.

"Hello, Mother," Luke said.

Eileen flushed. "Hello, Luke." She nodded toward Dayna. "Dayna." Her mouth turned down at the corners as she glanced at Jesse's arm. "I see you had a very exciting time camping."

"You could say that." Luke winked at Dayna. "We didn't know you had company."

Eileen's color deepened. "Todd and Jesse, why don't you go into the kitchen. I'm sure Bertha has some cookies and milk waiting for you."

Luke and Dayna shared a concerned look. Eileen never dismissed the boys so quickly. Usually she was the one hustling off with them to the kitchen for snacks. All four adults watched as the boys exited the room.

"Luke, Dayna," Eileen said, "I would like you to meet a very dear friend of mine, Lloyd Stephen Reinhold."

Lloyd stepped forward and shook their hands. "It's a pleasure to finally meet you two. I've heard so much about you and the boys."

Luke glanced between his mother and Lloyd. "I must admit you have us at a disadvantage."

"My fault entirely," Lloyd said. "I surprised Eileen five days ago when I showed up on her doorstep unannounced."

Luke stared at his mother, who refused to meet his eyes. "I'm obviously missing something here."

Lloyd went and stood next to Eileen's chair. "I

knew your mother years ago." He gave Eileen a tender smile. "We were more than just friends."

Dayna nudged Luke who only stood there blinking in confusion. He grunted, but still didn't seem to get it, so she said to Lloyd, "You were Steven's father, weren't you?"

"Yes."

Tears filled Eileen's eyes. "Lloyd didn't know I was pregnant with Steven when I sent him away. He didn't know he once had a son until five days ago."

Lloyd reached for her hands, raising them to his lips and kissing them. "Now I have two beautiful grandsons."

"Joseph Callahan wasn't Steven's father?" Luke had finally come to his senses and wasn't sure if he was happy about it or not. His mother had had an affair. An affair that had resulted in a child.

"I'm sorry, Luke." Tears rolled down Eileen's pale face, but for once she wasn't blubbering about her heart medicine and pleading for attention. She seemed sincerely troubled. "I was eighteen when my parents forced me to marry a man I didn't love, Joseph Callahan. You were born two days after my twentieth birthday. Before I could legally vote, your father had a string of mistresses, which suited me just fine. I had given him what he wanted, an heir to the Callahan empire. He had no further use for me besides being his hostess.

"Four years later, Lloyd walked into my life and stole my heart. I knew it was wrong, but I couldn't stop myself from loving him. When I found out I was pregnant, I sent Lloyd away because I was afraid Joseph would kill him."

"Why didn't you just leave my father?"

"Because years before Joseph had sworn he would never give me a divorce. He wasn't going to repeat Max's mistakes and hand out half the Callahan fortune to ex-wives." Eileen stood up and walked toward her son. "Can you ever forgive me?"

"For what?" He wasn't the one she had been unfaithful to. Two wrongs in his book never made a right.

"For being such a horrible mother to you. I took things out on you that you had no control over. I shouldn't have done that." She touched his cheek, but when his expression didn't soften, she let her hand fall. "You were forced on me by a man I didn't love. The day you were born I turned you over to a nurse, but I did love you. I was slowly realizing that when Lloyd entered my life, and I pushed you aside once again. When Steven was born, he looked so much like the man I loved that I lavished everything I had on him. Steven was all I had left of Lloyd, while you were the reminder of Joseph and the reason I could never be happy."

"Why didn't you go to Lloyd when Joseph died?" Dayna asked. It was a sad, heartbreaking story, with Luke as the main victim.

"I heard he'd gotten married and I was ashamed."

"I married a woman out of friendship," Lloyd said, "that grew into a sweet love. Not the kind of love I shared with Eileen, but a love nevertheless. She died last year after a lengthy illness." Lloyd walked over to Eileen and wrapped his arm around her shoulders, offering her all the support he could.

"Luke," he went on, "I've asked your mother to marry me and she has tentatively accepted my proposal on one condition."

"What's that?"

"That you give your blessing. She loves you very much, even though she's told me she has done nothing to prove that love."

Luke looked at his mother for the first time in years. Really looked. She appeared softer, happier, than he ever remembered seeing her. He couldn't imagine what her life with his father had been like. Probably a lot like Dayna's life with Steven. How could he refuse his mother happiness when his own had finally arrived? He looked at Lloyd. "My mother has the right to marry anyone she chooses. If she wishes that someone to be you, she has my blessing, for whatever it's worth. But I have one condition too."

"What's that?" Lloyd asked.

"That she realizes I have the right to marry anyone I choose."

"And that she realizes I have the same right," added Dayna.

Both Eileen and Lloyd watched as Luke took Dayna's hand and kissed it. Eileen shook her head. "Don't tell me!"

"Well," Luke said, "if you don't want to hear where your grandsons will be living . . ."

"Oh my Lord, you and Dayna." Her gaze shot back and forth between them. "I mean, Dayna and you." Her shocked expression turned to one of joy. "Really?"

Luke pulled Dayna against his side as the boys ran back into the room. Both were wearing milk mustaches and there were cookie crumbs all over Jesse's sling. "Really, Mother." He smiled as the boys attached themselves to his other side. Now for the hard part and to see just how repentant his mother really was. "We also decided that Dayna and the boys will be moving to my place in Virginia."

"All that way!" Eileen looked at Lloyd, who only raised an eyebrow, as if to say it was their life. She lifted her chin and graciously said, "That's wonderful, Luke. I'm sure Dayna and the boys will love it there." She looked at Dayna. "Would you two mind terribly if Lloyd and I visit once or twice a year?"

Dayna chuckled at Luke's expression. "We would love to have you, Eileen, and you, too, Lloyd, as often as you like. The boys have never had a grandfather before."

"A grandfather?" Todd asked. Both boys stared at Lloyd in fascination. "Are you really our grandfather?"

"It appears I am." He held out his hand. "Lloyd Reinhold's the name. But you two may call me Gramps."

"Do you know how to fish?" asked Jesse.

"No, but I've been meaning to take up the sport."

"I could teach you," Todd said, not wanting to be outdone by his brother.

Luke shook his head in amazement. He was just getting used to the idea of having two sons, and it appeared he was being shown up by a grandfather. His mother was getting married. He was getting married! Steven was only a half brother, and not really a Callahan at all. The amazing part was Eileen honestly looked regretful for the past. Hell, if this was Christmas, he would have to believe in miracles and Santa Claus.

He pulled Dayna from the room and out into the gardens. Lloyd, Eileen, and the boys were totally engrossed in discussing plans for a fishing trip in the near future.

Dayna laughed as he closed the French doors behind them. "Do you believe it? Steven wasn't a Callahan. The thing he flaunted the most wasn't even his to flaunt."

"It's only a name, Dayna. No better, no worse, than any other name."

"True. But to think I almost ran from you because of that name."

He pulled her away from the door and kissed her. "I'm glad you didn't."

"I think it's going to take a while to adjust to your mother getting married again."

"I think marriage is a wonderful institution. In fact, I'm planning on taking the plunge any day now.

Your couch is damn uncomfortable." He led her deeper into the garden. "I've been meaning to talk to you about something."

"Hmm . . ." She wrapped her arms around his neck and nuzzled his chin. "Can't it wait?"

"Nope." He chuckled at her attempt to reach his mouth. "You said that you wanted to stay home with the boys and only do substitute teaching for a couple of years."

"I said 'If we can afford it.' You're not getting an extra mouth to feed, you're getting three. And believe me, Todd and Jesse can pack away some food. I won't mention the cost of sneakers or needing new clothes every time they have a growth spurt."

He laughed. "I'm not worried about feeding and clothing all of you. And if you want to just substitute teach, that's fine by me."

"So what did you want to discuss with me?"

"What's your opinion on giving my mother another grandchild or two to spoil?"

Dayna smiled. "I always dreamed about having a daughter."

He backed her against a giant maple. "I'm going to make every one of your dreams come true."

"Every one?"

"Every one."

"Then the legend is true!"

"What legend?"

"The one about One-eyed Pete and that good things happen to those who see him." She brushed his mouth with a kiss. "The boys were hoping to strike gold."

"Ah . . . ." He pressed full length against her, leaving her with no doubt about his desire. "But we found something more precious than gold."

Her voice was a soft whisper as she lifted her mouth to his. "We found love."

THE EDITORS' CORNER

What do a cowboy, a straitlaced professor, a federal agent, and a wildlife photographer have in common? They're the sizzling men you'll meet in next month's LOVESWEPT lineup, and they're uniting with wonderful heroines for irresistible tales of passion and romance. Packed with emotion, these terrific stories are guaranteed to keep you enthralled. Enjoy!

Longtime romance favorite Karen Leabo begins the glorious BRIDES OF DESTINY series with **CALLIE'S COWBOY**, LOVESWEPT #806, a story of poignant magic, tender promises, and revealing truths. Sam Sanger had always planned to share his ranch and his future with Callie Calloway, but even in high school he understood that loving this woman might mean letting her go! When a fortune-teller hinted that her fate lay with Sam, Callie ran—afraid a life with Sam would mean sacrificing her dreams. Now, ten years later, she stops running long enough to wonder if Sam is the destiny she most desires. Displaying the style that has made her a #1 bestselling author, Karen Leabo explores the deep longings that lead us to love.

Warming hearts and tickling funny bones from start to finish, award-winner Jennifer Crusie creates her own fairy tale of love in **THE CINDERELLA DEAL**, LOVESWEPT #807. Linc Blaise needs the perfect fiancée to win his dream job, but finding a woman who'll be convincing in the charade seems impossible—until he hears Daisy Flattery charm her way out of a sticky situation! The bedazzling storyteller knows it'll be a snap playing a prim and proper lady to Linc's serious professor, but the pretense turns into a risky temptation when she discovers the vulnerable side Linc tries so hard to hide. Jennifer Crusie debuts in LOVESWEPT with an utterly charming story of opposites attracting.

Acclaimed author Laura Taylor provides a **SLIGHTLY SCANDALOUS** scenario for her memorable hero and heroine in her newest LOVE-SWEPT, #808. Trapped with a rugged stranger when a sudden storm stops an elevator between floors, Claire Duncan is shocked to feel the undeniable heat of attraction! In Tate Richmond she senses strength shadowed by a loneliness that echoes her own unspoken need. Vowing to explore the hunger that sparks between them, forced by unusual circumstances to resort to clandestine meetings, Tate draws her to him with tender ferocity. He has always placed honor above desire, kept himself safe in a world of constant peril, but once he's trusted his destiny to a woman of mystery, he can't live without her touch.

Laura Taylor packs quite a punch with this exquisite romance!

RaeAnne Thayne sets the mood with reckless passion and fierce destiny in **WILD STREAK,** LOVE-SWEPT #809. Keen Malone can't believe his ears when Meg O'Neill turns him down for a loan! Determined to make the cool beauty understand that his wildlife center is the mountain's only hope, he persuades her to tour the site. Meg can't deny the lush beauty of the land he loves, but how long can she fight the wild longing to run into his arms? RaeAnne Thayne creates a swirl of undeniable attraction in this classic romance of two strangers who discover they share the same fierce desire.

Happy reading!

With warmest wishes,

Beth de Guzman

Shauna Summers

Beth de Guzman   Shauna Summers

Senior Editor   Editor

P.S. Watch for these Bantam women's fiction titles coming in October. Praised by Amanda Quick as "an exciting find for romance readers everywhere," Elizabeth Elliott dazzles with **BETROTHED,** the much anticipated sequel to her debut novel, THE WAR-LORD. When Guy of Montague finds himself trapped in an engagement to Claudia, Baron Lonsdale's beautiful niece, his only thought is escape. But when she comes to his rescue, with the condition that he take her with him, he finds himself under her spell, willing to risk everything—even his life—to capture her heart. And don't miss **TAME THE WILD WIND** by Rosanne Bittner, the mistress of romantic frontier fiction. Half-breed Gabe Beaumont rides with a renegade Sioux band until a raid on a Wyoming stage post unites him with Faith Kelley. Together they will face their destinies and fight for their love against the shadows of their own wild hearts.

Be sure to see next month's LOVESWEPTs for a preview of these exceptional novels. And immediately following this page, preview the Bantam women's fiction titles on sale *now*!

Don't miss these extraordinary books
by your favorite Bantam authors

On sale in August:

AMANDA
by Kay Hooper

THE MARSHAL AND THE HEIRESS
by Patricia Potter

TEXAS LOVER
by Adrienne deWolfe

AMANDA

from bestselling author
Kay Hooper
now available in paperback

July, 1975

Thunder rolled and boomed, echoing the way it did when a storm came over the mountains on a hot night, and the wind-driven rain lashed the trees and furiously pelted the windowpanes of the big house. The nine-year-old girl shivered, her cotton night-gown soaked and clinging to her, and her slight body was stiff as she stood in the center of the dark bedroom.

"Mama—"

"Shhhh! Don't, baby, don't make any noise. Just stand there, very still, and wait for me."

They called her baby often, her mother, her father, because she'd been so difficult to conceive and was so cherished once they had her. So beloved. That was why they had named her Amanda, her father had explained, lifting her up to ride upon his broad shoulders, because she was so perfect and so worthy of their love.

She didn't feel perfect now. She felt cold and emptied out and dreadfully afraid. And the sound of her mother's voice, so thin and desperate, frightened Amanda even more. The bottom had fallen out of her world so suddenly that she was still numbly bewildered and broken, and her big gray eyes followed her mother with the piteous dread of one who had lost everything except a last fragile, unspeakably precious tie to what had been.

Whispering between rumbles of thunder, she asked, "Mama, where will we go?"

"Away, far away, baby." The only illumination in the bedroom was provided by angry nature as lightning split the stormy sky outside, and Christine Daulton used the flashes to guide her in stuffing clothes into an old canvas duffel bag. She dared not turn on any lights, and the need to hurry was so fierce it nearly strangled her.

She hadn't room for them, but she pushed her journals into the bag as well because she had to have *something* of this place to take with her, and something of her life with Brian. *Oh, dear God, Brian* . . . She raked a handful of jewelry from the box on the dresser, tasting blood because she was biting her bottom lip to keep herself from screaming. There was no time, no time, she had to get Amanda away from here.

"Wait here," she told her daughter.

"No! Mama, please—"

"Shhhh! All right, Amanda, come with me—but you have to be quiet." Moments later, down the hall in her daughter's room, Christine fumbled for more clothing and thrust it into the bulging bag. She helped the silent, trembling girl into dry clothing, faded jeans and a tee shirt. "Shoes?"

Amanda found a pair of dirty sneakers and shoved her feet into them. Her mother grasped her hand and led her from the room, both of them consciously tiptoeing. Then, at the head of the stairs, Amanda suddenly let out a moan of anguish and tried to pull her hand free. "Oh, I *can't*—"

"Shhhh," Christine warned urgently. "Amanda—"

Even whispering, Amanda's voice held a desperate intensity. "Mama, please, Mama, I have to get something—I can't leave it here, please, Mama—it'll only take a second—"

She had no idea what could be so precious to her daughter, but Christine wasn't about to drag her down the stairs in this state of wild agitation. The child was already in shock, a breath away from absolute hysteria. "All right, but hurry. And *be quiet.*"

As swift and silent as a shadow, Amanda darted back down the hallway and vanished into her bedroom. She reappeared less than a minute later, shoving something into the front pocket of her jeans. Christine didn't pause to find out what was so important that Amanda couldn't bear to leave it behind; she simply grabbed her daughter's free hand and continued down the stairs.

The grandfather clock on the landing whirred and bonged a moment before they reached it, announcing in sonorous tones that it was two A.M. The sound was too familiar to startle either of them, and they hurried on without pause. The front door was still open, as they'd left it, and Christine didn't bother to pull it shut behind them as they went through to the wide porch.

The wind had blown rain halfway over the porch to the door, and Amanda dimly heard her shoes squeak on the wet stone. Then she ducked her head against the rain and stuck close to her mother as they raced for the car parked several yards away. By the time she was sitting in the front seat watching her mother fumble with the keys, Amanda was soaked again and shivering, despite a temperature in the seventies.

The car's engine coughed to life, and its headlights stabbed through the darkness and sheeting rain to illuminate the graveled driveway. Amanda turned her head to the side as the car jolted toward the paved road, and she caught her breath when she saw a light bobbing far away between the house and the stables, as if someone was running with a flashlight. Running toward the car that, even then, turned onto the paved road and picked up speed as it left the house behind.

Quickly, Amanda turned her gaze forward again, rubbing her cold hands together, swallowing hard as sickness rose in her aching throat. "Mama? We can't come back, can we? We can't ever come back?"

The tears running down her ashen cheeks almost but not quite blinding her, Christine Daulton replied, "No, Amanda. We can't ever come back."

"One of the romance genre's finest talents."
—*Romantic Times*

From
Patricia Potter
bestselling author of *DIABLO*
comes

THE MARSHAL AND THE HEIRESS

When U.S. Marshal Ben Masters became Sarah Ann's guardian, he didn't know she was the lost heir to a Scottish estate—or that her life would soon be in danger. Now, instead of hunting down a gun-toting outlaw, he faces an aristocratic household bitterly divided by ambition. And not even falling in love with Sarah Ann's beautiful young aunt could keep her from being a suspect in Ben's eyes.

How do you tell a four-year-old girl that her mother is dead?

U.S. Marshal Ben Masters worried over the question as he stood on the porch of Mrs. Henrietta Culworthy's small house. Then, squaring his shoulders, he knocked. He wished he really believed he was doing the right thing. What in God's name did a man like him, a man who'd lived with guns and violence for the past eight years, have to offer an orphaned child?

Mary May believed in you. The thought raked through his heart. He felt partially responsible for her death. He had stirred a pot without considering the consequences. In bringing an end to an infamous outlaw hideout, he had been oblivious to those caught in the cross fire. The fact that Mary May had been involved with the outlaws didn't assuage his conscience.

Sarah. Promise you'll take care of Sarah. He would never forget Mary May's last faltering words.

Ben rapped again on the door of the house. Mrs. Culworthy should be expecting him. She had been looking after Sarah Ann for the past three years, but now she had to return east to care for a brother. She had already postponed her trip once, agreeing to wait until Ben had wiped out the last remnants of an outlaw band and fulfilled a promise to the former renegade named Diablo.

The door opened. Mrs. Culworthy's wrinkled face appeared, sagging slightly with relief. Had she worried that he would not return? He sure as hell had thought about it. He'd thought about a lot of things, like where he might find another suitable home for Sarah Ann. But then he would never be sure she was being raised properly. By God, he owed Mary May.

"Sarah Ann?" he asked Mrs. Culworthy.

"In her room." The woman eyed him hopefully. "You *are* going to take her."

He nodded.

"What about your job?"

"I'm resigning. I used to be a lawyer. Thought I would hang up my shingle in Denver."

A smile spread across Mrs. Culworthy's face. "Thank heaven for you. I love that little girl. I would take her if I could, but—"

"I know you would," he said gently. "But she'll be safe with me." He hoped that was true. He hesitated. "She doesn't know yet, does she? About her mother?"

Mrs. Culworthy shook her head.

Just then, a small head adorned with reddish curls

and green eyes peered around the door. Excitement lit the gamin face. "Mama's here!"

Pain thrust through Ben. Of course, Sarah Ann would think her mother had arrived. Mary May had been here with him just a few weeks ago.

"Uncle Ben," the child said, "where's Mama?"

He wished Mrs. Culworthy had already told her. He was sick of being the bearer of bad news, and never more so than now.

He dropped to one knee and held out a hand to the little girl. "She's gone to heaven," Ben said.

She approached slowly, her face wrinkling in puzzlement; then she looked questioningly at Mrs. Culworthy. The woman dissolved into tears. Ben didn't know whether Sarah Ann understood what was being said, but she obviously sensed that something was very wrong. The smile disappeared and her underlip started to quiver.

Ben's heart quaked. He had guarded that battered part of him these past years, but there were no defenses high enough, or thick enough, to withstand a child's tears.

He held out his arms, not sure Sarah Ann knew him well enough to accept his comfort. But she walked into his embrace, and he hugged her, stiffly at first. Unsure. But then her need overtook his uncertainty, and his grip tightened.

"You asked me once if I were your papa," he said. "Would you like me to be?"

Sarah Ann looked up at him. "Isn't Mama coming back?"

He shook his head. "She can't, but she loved you so much she asked me to take care of you. If that's all right with you?"

Sarah Ann turned to Mrs. Culworthy. "I want to stay with you, Cully."

"You can't, Pumpkin," Mrs. Culworthy said tenderly. "I have to go east, but Mr. Masters will take good care of you. Your mother thought so, too."

"Where is heaven? Can't I go, too?"

"Someday," Ben said slowly. "And she'll be waiting for you, but right now I need you. I need someone to take care of me, too, and your mama thought we could take care of each other."

It was true, he suddenly realized. He did need someone to love. His life had been empty for so long.

Sarah Ann probably had much to offer him.

But what did he have to offer her?

Sarah Ann put her hand to his cheek. The tiny fingers were incredibly soft—softer than anything he'd ever felt—and gentle. She had lost everything, yet she was comforting him.

He hugged her close for a moment, and then he stood. Sarah Ann's hand crept into his. Trustingly. And Ben knew he would die before ever letting anything bad happen to her again.

TEXAS LOVER

by

Adrienne deWolfe

author of *TEXAS OUTLAW*

To Texas Ranger Wes Rawlins, settling a property dispute should be no trickier than peeling potatoes—even if it does involve a sheriff's cousin and a headstrong schoolmarm on opposite camps. But Wes quickly learns there's more to the matter than meets the eye. The only way to get at the truth is from the inside. So posing as a carpenter, the lawman uncovers more than he bargains for in a feisty beauty and her house full of orphans.

"Sons of thunder."

Rorie rarely resorted to such unladylike outbursts, but the strain of her predicament was wearing on her. She had privately conceded she could not face Hannibal Dukker with the same laughable lack of shooting skill she had displayed for Wes Rawlins. So, swallowing her great distaste for guns—and the people who solved their problems with them—she had forced herself to ride out to the woods early, before the children arrived for their lessons, to practice her marksmanship.

It was a good thing she had done so.

She had just fired her sixth round, her *sixth round*, for heaven's sake, and that abominable whiskey bottle still sat untouched on the top of her barrel. If she had been a fanciful woman—which she most assuredly was not—she might have imagined that impudent vessel was trying to provoke her. Why, it hadn't rattled once when her bullets whizzed by. And the long rays of morning sun had fired it a bright and frolicsome green. If there was one thing she couldn't abide, it was a frolicsome whiskey bottle.

Her mouth set in a grim line, she fished in the pocket of her pinafore for more bullets.

Thus occupied, Rorie didn't immediately notice the tremor of the earth beneath her boots. She didn't ascribe anything unusual to her nag's snorting or the way Daisy stomped her hoof and tossed her head. The beast was chronically fractious.

Soon, though, Rorie detected the sound of thrashing, as if a powerful animal were breaking through the brush around the clearing. Her heart quickened, but she tried to remain calm. After all, bears were hardly as brutish as their hunters liked to tell. And any other wild animal with sense would turn tail and run once it got wind of her human scent—not to mention a whiff of her gunpowder.

Still, it might be wise to start reloading. . . .

A bloodcurdling whoop shook her hands. She couldn't line up a single bullet with its chamber. She thought to run, but there was nowhere to hide, and Daisy was snapping too viciously to mount.

Suddenly the sun winked out of sight. A horse, a *mammoth* horse with fiery eyes and steaming nostrils, sailed toward her over the barrel. She tried to scream, but it lodged in her throat as an "eek." All she could do was stand there, jaw hanging, knees knocking, and remember the unfortunate schoolmaster, Ichabod Crane.

Only her horseman had a head.

A red head, to be exact. And he carried it above his shoulders, rather than tucked under his arm.

"God a'mighty! Miss Aurora!"

The rider reined in so hard that his gelding reared, shrilling in indignation. Her revolver slid from her fingers. She saw a peacemaker in the rider's fist, and she thought again about running.

"It's me, ma'am. Wes Rawlins," he called, then cursed as his horse wheeled and pawed.

She blinked uncertainly, still poised to flee. He didn't look like the dusty longrider who'd drunk from her well the previous afternoon. His hair was sleek and short, and his cleft chin was bare of all but morning stubble. Although he did still wear the mustache, it was the gunbelt that gave him away. She recognized the double holsters before she recognized his strong, sculpted features.

He managed to subdue his horse before it could bolt back through the trees. "Are you all right, ma'am?" He hastily dismounted, releasing his reins to ground-hitch the gelding. "Uh-oh." He peered into her face. "You aren't gonna faint or anything, are you?"

She snapped erect, mortified by the very suggestion. "Certainly not. I've never been sick a day in my life. And swooning is for invalids."

"Sissies, too," he agreed solemnly.

He ran an appreciative gaze over her hastily piled hair and down her crisply pressed pinafore to her mud-spattered boots. She felt the blood surge to her cheeks. Masking her discomfort, she planted both fists on her hips.

"*Mister* Rawlins. What on earth is the matter with you, tearing around the countryside like that? You frightened the devil out of my horse!"

"I'm real sorry, ma'am. I never meant to give

your, er, *horse* such a fright. But you see, I heard gun-shots. And since there's nothing out this way except the Boudreau homestead, I thought you might be having trouble."

"Trouble?" She felt her heart flutter. Had he heard something of Dukker's intentions?

"Well, sure. Yesterday, the way you had those children running for cover, I thought you might be expecting some." He folded his arms across his chest. "Are you?"

The directness of his question—and his gaze—was unsettling. He no longer reminded her of a lion. To-day he was a fox, slick and clever, with a dash of sly charm thrown in to confuse her. She hastily bolstered her defenses.

"Did it ever occur to you, Mr. Rawlins, that Shae might be out here shooting rabbits?"

"Nope. Never thought I'd find you here, either. Not that I mind, ma'am. Not one bit. You see, I'm the type who likes surprises. Especially pleasant ones."

She felt her face grow warmer. She wasn't used to flattery. Her husband had been too preoccupied with self-pity to spare many kind words for her in the last two years of their marriage.

"Well," she said, "I never expected to see you out here either, Mr. Rawlins."

"Call me Wes."

She forced herself to ignore his winsome smile. "In truth, sir, I never thought to see you again."

"Why's that?"

"Let's be honest, Mr. Rawlins. You are no carpen-ter."

He chuckled. She found herself wondering which had amused him more: her accusation or her refusal to use his Christian name.

"You have to give a feller a chance, Miss Aurora. You haven't even seen my handiwork yet."

"I take it you've worked on barns before?"

"Sure. Fences too. My older brothers have a ranch up near Bandera Pass. Zack raises cattle. Cord raises kids. I try to raise a little thunder now and then, but they won't let me." He winked. "That's why I had to ride south."

She felt a smile tug at her lips. She was inclined to believe a part of his story, the part about him rebelling against authority.

"You aren't gonna make me bed down again in these woods, are you, ma'am? 'Cause Two-Step is awful fond of hay."

He managed to look woeful, in spite of the impish humor lighting his eyes. She realized then just how practiced his roguery was. Wary again, she searched his gaze, trying to find some hint of the truth. Why hadn't he stayed at the hotel in town? Or worse, at the dance hall? She felt better knowing he hadn't spent his free time exploiting an unfortunate young whore, but she still worried that his reasons for sleeping alone had more to do with empty pockets than any nobility of character. What would Rawlins do if Dukker offered to hire his guns?

Maybe feeding and housing Rawlins was more prudent than driving him off. Boarding him could steer him away from Dukker's dangerous influence, and Shae could genuinely use the help on the barn.

"Very well, Mr. Rawlins. I shall withhold judgment on your carpentry skills until you've had a chance to prove yourself."

"Why, that's right kind of you, ma'am."

She felt her cheeks grow warm again. His lilting drawl had the all-too-disturbing tendency to make her feel uncertain and eighteen again.

"I suppose you'll want to ride on to the house now," she said. "It's a half-mile farther west. Shae is undoubtedly awake and can show you what to do." She inclined her head. "Good morning."

Except for a cannily raised eyebrow, he didn't budge.

Rorie fidgeted. She was unused to her dismissals going unheeded. She was especially unused to a young man regarding her as if she had just made the most delightful quip of the season.

Hoping he would go away if she ignored him, she stooped to retrieve her gun. He reached quickly to help. She was so stunned when he crouched before her, his corded thighs straining beneath the fabric of his blue jeans, that she leaped up, nearly butting her head against his. He chuckled.

"Do I make you nervous, ma'am?"

"Certainly not." Her ears burned at the lie. "Whatever makes you think that?"

"Well . . ." Still squatting, he scooped bullets out of the bluebonnets that rose like sapphire spears around her hem. "I was worried you might be trying to get rid of me again."

"I—I only thought that Shae was expecting you," she stammered, hastily backing away. There was something disconcerting—not to mention titillating—about a man's bronzed fingers snaking through the grass and darting so near to the unmentionables one wore beneath one's skirt.

"Shae's not expecting me yet, ma'am. The sun's too low in the sky." Rawlins straightened leisurely. "I figure I've got a half hour, maybe more, before I report to the barn. Just think, Miss Aurora, that gives us plenty of time to get acquainted."

On sale in September:

TAME THE WILD HEART

by Rosanne Bittner

BETROTHED

by Elizabeth Elliott

DON'T MISS THESE FABULOUS
BANTAM WOMEN'S FICTION TITLES

On Sale in August

Available in mass market

AMANDA

from bestselling author *Kay Hooper*

"*Amanda* seethes and sizzles. A fast-paced atmospheric tale that
vibrates with tension, passion, and mystery."

—CATHERINE COULTER

____ 56823-X $5.99/$7.99 Canada

THE MARSHAL AND THE HEIRESS

by *Patricia Potter*

"One of the romance genre's finest talents." —*Romantic Times*

The bestselling author of *Diablo* captivates with a western lawman lassoing the bad guys—in Scotland! ____ 57508-2 $5.99/$7.99

from *Adrienne deWolfe*
the author *Romantic Times* touted as
"an exciting new talent" comes

TEXAS LOVER

Texas Ranger Wes Rawlins comes up against the barrel of a shot-
gun held by a beautiful Yankee woman with a gaggle of orphans
under her care.   ____ 57481-7 $5.50/$7.50